A YULETIDE PUZZLE . . .
FEATURING A SNOWBOUND EVENING AT A COUNTRY
INN . . . AND A CORPSE (OF COURSE).
BUT BE WARNED! THE CLUES ARE *MURDER* . . .

Soft light filled the chapel, and revealed that Maria had been right. There was a special, personal surprise for them.

It took the form of a dead body.

The dead man lay between the front pews and the altar. On the wall above him could be seen the discoloured cobwebbed outline of the shield which had fallen to kill him.

It lay face down, obscuring the man's head.

A steely resignation came into Jack Tarrant's eye. "The murderer is playing games with us, Maria."

He suddenly leant forward in the wheelchair and looked minutely at the back of the shield. "And that could be a part of those games."

"What?" She looked curiously down as he pointed out a grid of pencil lines on the old discoloured metal of the shield's back. "What do those mean?"

"I don't know yet, but they mean something. We're up against someone for whom every detail means something."

"Are you saying the murderer is actually setting up clues for us to find?"

"Exactly that, Maria. He's pitting his wits against ours. He's challenging us."

AND NOW WE'RE CHALLENGING *YOU* TO SOLVE . . .

THE CHRISTMAS CRIMES AT PUZZEL MANOR

Simon Brett
THE
CHRISTMAS CRIMES
AT PUZZEL MANOR

A Dell Trade Paperback

DEDICATED TO THE DEVIOUS
(Including Alastair, with thanks for his help)

A DELL TRADE PAPERBACK

Published by
Dell Publishing
a division of
Bantam Doubleday Dell Publishing Group, Inc.
1540 Broadway
New York, New York 10036

This work was first published in Great Britain by Coronet Books, Hodder & Stoughton Ltd.

The characters and situations in this book are entirely imaginary and bear no relation to any real person or actual happenings.

ISBN: 0-440-50469-4

Reprinted by arrangement with Delacorte Press

Printed in the United States of America

December 1993

10 9 8 7 6 5 4 3 2 1

RRH

PER INGENIUM AD SOLUTIONEM

PUZZEL MANOR
LUXURY TRADITIONAL CHRISTMAS BREAK

Recapture the Christmas spirit of an earlier and more elegant age in the historic surroundings of Puzzel Manor, a beautifully restored eighteenth century Country House, nestling in the folds of the Cotswolds near the quaint English village of Puzzel Moultby. Combining the latest in modern amenities with a respect for heritage, the hotel has recently under-gone extensive refurbishment under the skilled direction of its owners, Roddy and Jan Stout, for whom the comfort of their guests has always been the first priority. The Puzzel Manor kitchens are under the direction of award-winning Danish chef, Anders Altmidson, ensuring an unrivalled gastronomic experience over the Christmas break. Guests who prefer to relax are quite at liberty to do so, but for the more active, a full programme of events and entertainments has been arranged to ensure forty-eight hours of conviviality – a Christmas you will never forget!

PROGRAMME:

CHRISTMAS EVE:	Afternoon	Arrival
	6.00 p.m.	Ice-breaking Reception
	10.00 p.m.	Ghost Story
	11.30 p.m.	Midnight Mass in the Puzzel Chapel
CHRISTMAS DAY:	12.30 a.m.	Mince Pies and Nightcap
	8.00 a.m.	Stocking Opening
	1.30 p.m.	Traditional Christmas Lunch
	6.00 p.m.	Dickens by the Fireside
	8.30 p.m.	Party Games – "Murder in the Dark", etc.
	11.00 p.m.	Christmas Cake and Nightcap
BOXING DAY:	10.00 a.m.	Country Walk
	12.30 p.m.	Stirrup Cup with the Local Hunt
	Afternoon	Departure

HOW TO GET TO PUZZEL MANOR

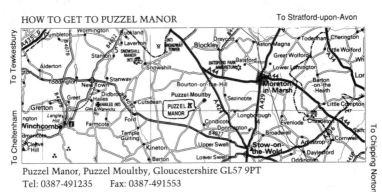

Puzzel Manor, Puzzel Moultby, Gloucestershire GL57 9PT
Tel: 0387-491235   Fax: 0387-491553

ONE

CHRISTMAS EVE – AFTERNOON. ARRIVAL

"Well, I'd say this was a bit of all right," said Jack Tarrant, formerly of Scotland Yard, as he heaved himself out of his wheelchair, hovered for a moment, supported on his strong arms, and then flopped on to the yellow quilted coverlet of the four-poster bed.

He looked round the Yellow Room of Puzzel Manor. The emulsioned walls glowed like French mustard, and the same tone was echoed in the stripe of the curtains that hung profusely round the four-poster and framed the formal eighteenth-century squares of the window panes. Through these, snow could be seen, suddenly caught in the spill of light, still falling relentlessly, as it had done all day.

From where he lay, he could see the comforting orange of the open fire reflected in the windows. Points of flame also winked back from the polished brass of the fire-irons, the dark oak of dresser, wardrobe and four-poster, the gleaming skins of fruit in a basket on a low fireside table, the ice bucket, the gold foil on the champagne bottle, and the two tall flutes that stood beside it.

"No, they've really done us proud," he continued.

"I'll say," Maria Lethbury purred from the fireside. She still wore moonboots, had her duvet coat wrapped around her and woolly hat pulled down almost to her chocolate brown eyes, as if unwilling to believe that she really was in from the cold.

1

Jack looked across, once again amazed at his good fortune in having her. Maria Lethbury really was the product of that old music hall pairing, a bishop and an actress. From her father she had inherited a cool, analytical mind and basic moral seriousness, while her mother had contributed flaming red hair, irreverent frivolity and an uncomplicated relish for sex. Maria Lethbury's father could always be recognised at Synod because he was the bishop who was smiling.

And now Jack Tarrant found he was smiling, too. Even swaddled as she was, Maria didn't lose her sexiness. And she was clever. Running her own Public Relations business in her late twenties. Making good money, successful. He could never really understand what she'd seen in him *before* the accident, and now her love seemed even more incongruous . . .

Still, some things just shouldn't be questioned. Accept what you've got with gratitude, Jack Tarrant told himself not for the first time.

He looked with satisfaction around the Yellow Room, then reached up his arms behind his head, with an automatic wince at the pain the movement triggered in his shattered hip.

"No, I think we could have a very good Christmas."

His voice, Maria noticed with satisfaction, already sounded more relaxed than it had for months. Even the hard lines of his thin face and the wrinkles round his grey eyes looked a little less taut, as he went on, "So, many thanks to our benefactors, eh? I have to say, before this came up, I'd never even heard of the Police Injuries Subscription Society."

"Nor had I, but it doesn't surprise me. One of the by-products of being a bishop's daughter is that you discover there are more charities in the world than you ever thought possible."

Maria saw the shadow that crossed Jack's face, and instantly regretted her use of the word "charity". He was still very touchy on such matters. She knew, better than anyone, how deeply it had hurt Jack to have his career as a detective cut short at the age of thirty-five by a villain's bullet.

He'd been offered a desk-job, of course, but that wasn't Jack Tarrant's style. If he couldn't be in the thick of the scrum, there was no way he was going to watch from the touchline. No, once he was finally out of hospital, bored to tears and having solved every crossword puzzle that could be thrown at him, he'd resigned from the Force, determined to make his career as something other than a policeman. As yet, that something hadn't materialised.

Maria was so pleased that she had managed to persuade him to come to Puzzel Manor. When the letter from the Police Injuries Subscription Society had first arrived, offering the expenses-paid package for two, Jack's pride would not allow him to accept. The whole thing smelt of patronage. Jack Tarrant wasn't going to take something he hadn't earned.

Winning him round to the idea had exercised all Maria's powers of persuasion – and those were considerable, combining as they did her father's skills in argument and rhetoric, together with her mother's more direct methods. Maria had itemised all the achievements of Jack's career as a Detective-Inspector, listed villains trapped, murderers unmasked.

She had not, however, dwelt at length on his final case – the pursuit of a cunning psychopath dubbed by the tabloid press, with characteristic fastidiousness, "The Executive Exterminator".

This killer had been so named because of his choice of victims – all successful businesswomen in their late twenties or early thirties. The fact that all six who died had been notably attractive had appealed to the tabloids, who usually managed to drag up a bikini-clad holiday snap of the victim to titillate their readers.

Jack Tarrant was just glad the papers never found out the precise details of the killer's murder methods – they would have really had a field day with those.

He had been close to trapping the monster, so very close. Like many such psychopaths, "The Executive Exterminator" was an exhibitionist. He prided himself on his cleverness and enjoyed the fact that the investigating authorities always seemed to limp a few paces behind him. So he started to show off, taunting the police, challenging them to catch him.

And Jack Tarrant played on this weakness in his quarry. He started to set up his own challenges and was rewarded by a response from the killer. The two had circled each other, unseen, in a deadly game of chess until finally, one night outside a converted Docklands warehouse, they had almost met. Certainly been close enough to meet. Close enough, at least, for "The Executive Exterminator" to shoot at his dogged pursuer, to fire into Jack Tarrant the bullet that was to smash his hip and end his Scotland Yard career.

The Detective-Inspector had not seen his adversary, but, at the moment he was blinded by the pain in his thigh, he had heard a laugh, a light, mocking laugh that still echoed agonisingly inside his head. That laugh was the sound to which he woke up sweating in the middle of the night. That laugh he was afraid, like the postoperative scars on his hip, would stay with him for the rest of his life.

Jack Tarrant had seemed to hear the laugh again when he came round in hospital to the news that, after shooting his hunter, "The Executive Exterminator" had calmly gone into the converted warehouse, found the apartment of his sixth carefully targeted victim, and despatched her with the same callous atrocity he had shown to the other five.

Jack was left with the bitter knowledge that, not only had his adversary ended Jack Tarrant's career as a detective, but he had also ensured that that career had ended on a note of defeat.

So Maria Lethbury did not mention "The Executive Exterminator" when she won Jack round to the idea of accepting the Christmas offer. But the unspoken knowledge hung between them. Maria had witnessed too many of her lover's nightmares to imagine he could ever forget.

She removed her hat, slipped out of her coat, kicked off the moonboots, arched her back and stretched upwards, like a contented cat. "Oh, look, there's a coat of arms above the fireplace."

"The Puzzel Arms," Jack confirmed. "As plastered all over the stationery of Puzzel Manor. And as on the inn-sign of the local hostelry in Puzzel Moultby. Everything round here used to belong to the Puzzel family."

"Been reading guide-books again, haven't you, Jack?"

"Always believe in doing a bit of research before going somewhere new."

"Very odd name, isn't it? Puzzel."

4

"Mm. Norman-French. First Puzzels came over with the Conqueror. Though then the name was 'Pucelle'."

"Meaning 'maiden' or 'virgin'." Maria's expensive education never let her down on such matters. "As in 'Jeanne la Pucelle' . . . 'La Pucelle d'Orléans' – Joan of Arc."

"That's it."

"Hm." Her chocolate brown eyes flickered across to the windows. "Snow's thicker than ever. We'd never have made it by road."

"No, I'd written the whole jaunt off when I saw the weather this morning. Couldn't believe it when we had that call saying they were laying on a helicopter."

"It just goes to show," said Maria, "how much respect you still command. I think this whole thing is Scotland Yard, in one of its rare graceful moments, saying, 'Thank you for everything, Jack Tarrant.'"

He didn't believe it, but he was flattered by the idea. With a wry smile, he said, "Why not pretend that's true. Get the holiday off to a good start, eh?"

Maria picked up the bottle of champagne. "This could help, too. Are you thirsty, by any chance, Jack?"

"Can't use the old 'Not while I'm on duty' line, can I? Since I never am on duty these days."

She looked across sharply, but saw he was joking rather than bitter. With relief she slipped her nail under the foil of the champagne bottle.

Jack's grey eyes turned back to the window. "Nobody else is going to get here now. I should think this weather's hit their bookings pretty hard."

"Apparently not. The girl at Reception said most of the guests have already arrived."

"Pretty girl who checked us in?"

"Yes."

"'NERYS – Assistant Manager', according to her lapel badge."

"That's right. I had a word with her while the helicopter co-pilot was wheeling you in."

"And she's the only person we've met so far." He picked up a copy of the "Christmas Break" brochure and glanced at it. "Still,

5

no doubt we'll see the rest at the 'Ice-breaking Reception' at six o'clock."

"Literally ice-breaking, in this weather." Maria brought two glasses of champagne across to the four-poster. "How do you fancy being snowed in, Jack Tarrant?"

"Can't think of anyone I'd rather be snowed in with, Maria Lethbury. I hope that –" he consulted the brochure – "the 'award-winning Danish chef Anders Altmidson' has got a well-stocked larder."

"I'm sure he has."

Maria lay down on the quilt and snuggled against him. "This is perfect, I'd say. Perfect room. The only bedroom on the ground floor, which couldn't be more convenient."

"For the disabled, you mean?"

The hurt was suddenly back in his voice.

"No," she soothed. "I didn't mean that, Jack. I just meant this room is very convenient."

He still looked bitter.

"Look, there's not going to be any problem about you getting round the place. The public rooms are all on the ground floor. And there's a lift, anyway. I noticed in the plan they gave us."

She took up a folded sheet from the bedside table. As she did so, a slip of paper fluttered out on to the quilt between them.

Jack picked it up. It was a Puzzel Manor "With Compliments" slip, with the coat of arms embossed in the top left-hand corner and another motif in the bottom right.

"Oh, we are privileged, Maria. We've got something before the six o'clock 'Ice-breaking Reception'."

"What?" she asked languorously.

He read out the handwritten message. "'Jack and Maria, the fun starts for you in the Chapel at half-past five.'"

"No, it doesn't," said Maria, purposefully reaching for the loose end of Jack's belt. "It starts here. Now."

He chuckled, as his hand found her thigh and ran gently up its silken contour. "You know, this is the only time I completely forget about my injury. I feel a whole man again."

"That's exactly what *I'm* doing – feeling a whole man," said the bishop's daughter – well, no, to be accurate, at that moment she was more the actress's daughter. "You know," she murmured, "I'll never get over the relief that that bullet didn't go a few inches to the left."

"Doesn't bear thinking of."

She nuzzled closer. He looked up at the windows.

"Should we draw the curtains? We are on the ground floor, after all."

"Jack . . . nobody's going to be out in that lot. We could turn off the lights, though."

They did.

"Oh, Maria . . ."

"Oh, Jack . . ."

Firelight rippled against the ceiling and illuminated the swirling snowflakes which still fell, thick and bloated, outside the windows of Puzzel Manor.

The corridors were wide enough for the wheelchair, and Jack Tarrant propelled himself expertly along, spinning the wheels with strong economical strokes. Maria walked a little behind, tactfully not offering to push. Her cheeks glowed and eyes sparkled after their recent exertions.

"According to the guide-book I read," said Jack, "there's an old metal shield in the chapel. Late medieval, I think. Painted with the Puzzel coat of arms. One should not pay a visit to the house without seeing it."

"Then we certainly will see it."

"Been chained to the wall for centuries. The legend has it that the shield protects the Puzzel family and, if ever that shield is moved, disaster will strike them."

Maria chuckled. "Must've been moved then, I should think. The Puzzels've died out, haven't they?"

"Don't know."

"Well, at least they no longer own the place. I don't imagine that Roddy and Jan Stout are related to the Puzzels, do you?"

"Pretty unlikely, I should think. Here we are."

They had reached a fire door, on which was a notice reading "TO THE CHAPEL".

The building was of considerably older date than the Manor House itself. Jack's guide-book spoke of Saxon foundations, and the Cotswold stone had weathered to a beautifully soft grey.

It was joined to the house by a short covered passage, illuminated by one meagre electric bulb. Along the sides, unlit candles stood in their holders, ready to light the way of the guests who wished to celebrate the advertised Midnight Mass later in the evening.

Jack made no demur as Maria moved ahead to grasp the iron ring of the chapel's heavy oak doors. She pulled them open. The interior was in darkness. "See if I can find a light-switch," she said, as she went down a shallow step and disappeared into the gloom.

"Strange there's no one here." Jack pulled the "With Compliments" slip out of his pocket to recheck the message. "It's after half-past five."

He took a closer look at the strange design in the bottom right-hand corner of the paper, and wondered idly what it signified.

"Maybe the 'fun' we're promised doesn't involve any other people," Maria's voice suggested from the gloom. "Maybe there's just some kind of special, personal surprise for us in here. Maybe – ah, found it!"

Soft light filled the chapel, and revealed that Maria had been right. There was a special, personal surprise for them.

It took the form of a dead body.

Jack Tarrant instantly shoved the "With Compliments" slip back into his pocket. His wheelchair clattered down the step and sped along the smooth stone aisle to where the corpse lay.

The Puzzel Manor chapel was small, with a few narrow stained glass windows at the altar end. The walls were covered with heraldic memorials to long-dead members of the Puzzel family. Above the pulpit was a wooden hymn indicator board, though there were no numbers in its slots.

The dead man lay to one side, between the front pews and the altar. On the wall above him, over a little ledge on which the Puzzel motto was carved, could be seen the discoloured cob-webbed outline of the shield which had fallen to kill him.

It lay face down, obscuring the man's head. Two halves of its chain hung from rings on each side. At the end of one was a broken link.

Gripping the arms of his wheelchair for purchase, Jack Tarrant used the toecap of his good leg to lift the edge of the shield, and looked underneath.

There was surprisingly little blood, but the man's head was crushed and elongated. His mouth had been forced slightly open. Together with his staring eyes, this gave him an expression of affronted surprise. Which, under the circumstances, was quite justified.

He was probably in his late fifties. His hair had that almost translucent whiteness which age brings to the very blond. Plumpish, he wore a nondescript, crumpled dark grey suit and a very new-looking clergyman's collar.

"Must be the local vicar," Maria murmured. "Presumably getting things ready for the Midnight Mass, and had the misfortune to be standing underneath at the moment the chain finally rusted through."

"No," said Jack Tarrant, once again lowering the Puzzel shield on to its victim.

"No?"

"If he was getting things ready, he would have had the lights on. And –" he turned the broken end of the chain with his foot to reveal the silver gleam of a sheared-off link – "that didn't rust. It was sawn or cut through. What we're looking at here is a case of murder."

"But why – ?"

"What's more, it's a case of murder which we were meant to find. That's why we were summoned to the chapel." A steely resignation came into Jack Tarrant's eye. "The murderer is playing games with us, Maria."

He suddenly leant forward in the wheelchair and looked minutely at the back of the shield. "And that could be a part of those games."

"What?" She looked curiously down as he pointed out a grid of pencil lines on the old discoloured metal of the shield's back. "What do those mean?"

"I don't know yet, but they mean something. We're up against someone for whom every detail means something."

"Are you saying that the murderer is actually setting up clues for us to find?"

"Exactly that, Maria. He's pitting his wits against ours. He's challenging us."

There was a grimness in Jack Tarrant's tone as he said this, but also a fierce undercurrent of excitement. He had identified the challenge and there was no way he wasn't going to take it up.

"Check his pockets, love." Then, with sudden sensitivity, he added, "Do you mind?"

"No." The bishop and actress's daughter was not going to give in to squeamishness. She knelt down and, with cool efficiency, started to go through the dead man's pockets.

As she did so, Maria Lethbury sniffed with distaste. "Horrible smell of mothballs."

Jack Tarrant felt the corpse's hand. "Goodness, he's cold. Very, very cold." Then he once again took the "With Compliments" slip out of his pocket and studied it with intense concentration.

"You reckon there's a clue in that too, Jack?"

"I'm certain of it." A grim smile came to his lips. "And I think I can see how it's hidden."

He reached into his inside pocket, producing a pencil and a copy of the Puzzel Manor Christmas Break brochure. He looked at the latter, then at the "With Compliments" slip, and nodded.

"Oh yes. The answer is one word of four letters. I'm sure there'll be worse to come, but he's starting us off with an easy one."

And Jack Tarrant wrote down the solution to the first Puzzel Manor puzzle.

With Compliments

JACK + MARIA

The fun starts for you
in the Chapel
at half-past
five!

PER INGENIAM AD SOLUTIONEM

Puzzel Manor, Puzzel Moultby, Gloucestershire GL57 9PT
Tel: 0387 - 13 2 10 3   Fax: 0387 - 491553

TWO

CHRISTMAS EVE –
6.00 P.M. ICE-BREAKING
RECEPTION

"What's going on here?"

They turned to the doorway at the sound of the voice. Maria, who had just found a notebook in the pocket of the corpse's jacket, neatly palmed and slipped it up the voluminous sleeve of her woollen dress.

"I saw the lights were on. What's happened?"

The speaker was tall, in his early fifties, with thinning gingerish hair and blotchy patches of purple on his cheeks. He was dressed in the corduroy trousers, beige waistcoat and tweed jacket of a country gentleman, and his slightly languid, upper class accent supported the impression.

"Someone's dead," said Jack Tarrant tersely.

"What!" The man moved swiftly down the aisle until he could see the sprawled clergyman. "My God, who is he? And who are you two, come to that?"

"Jack Tarrant." He still had to bite his lip to hold back the automatic prefix of "Detective-Inspector".

"Maria Lethbury."

The man, incongruously formal given the circumstances, stretched out a hand to each of them in turn. "I'm Roddy Stout, the proprietor here. Welcome to Puzzel Manor."

Then he turned his attention to the corpse. His reaction was one of being hugely inconvenienced rather than shocked by this loss of a human life. "Any idea who it is?"

"He's wearing a dog-collar. He died here in the chapel. Might mean he's some sort of clergyman."

"The Rev. Verdure," Roddy Stout pronounced. "Must be. Oh God, this is inconvenient! First the bloody weather – and now this! Just the start we *didn't* need. We've put so much work into organising this Christmas Break."

"Can you make a positive identification of the deceased?" asked Jack Tarrant, dropping instinctively into his former role.

"Well, no I can't, but it must be him."

"Why can't you identify him?"

"Because I've never met him. We've only spoken on the phone. You see, the Rev. Verdure is – *was* the local parish priest in Puzzel Moultby. The vicarage is just by the main gates of the Manor. You'd have seen it as you drove in."

"We arrived by helicopter."

"Oh, you were the ones, right. Sorry I wasn't around to welcome you then. Tied up sorting out some details with the chef. Actually we'd written you off. Heard on the radio that both the A424 and the B4077 were impassable with snow."

"Have many of your guests not been able to make it?"

"No, we've been pretty lucky, actually. Only one absentee, as it turns out. Most arrived yesterday, or early this morning before conditions got so bad."

"Sorry, Mr Stout, you were saying . . . about the vicar?"

"Oh, right, yes. As I say, he runs the parish of Puzzel Moultby. It's a small place, so it's not really a full-time job, but he's semi-retired, apparently, so it suits him.

"Anyway, afraid I'm not much of a church-goer myself – nor's my wife Jan – but when we were planning this Christmas Break, we knew that some people might want a bit of a religious element, so I rang up the Rev. Verdure and asked if he'd agree to conduct a Midnight Mass here in the chapel. He hummed and hawed a bit, but since the Puzzel Moultby Carol Service happens early evening on Christmas Eve, he couldn't really say no."

A thought made Roddy Stout glance at his watch. "Oh dear. If he's dead, there isn't going to be a Carol Service in Puzzel Moultby, is there? I'd better let someone in the village know."

Jack Tarrant wasn't impressed by this sense of priorities. "And you'd better let the police know too."

"Yes. Yes, of course." But the hotelier didn't sound very convinced. "You don't suppose we could, sort of, leave it for forty-eight hours, do you . . . ? I mean, we've put a hell of a lot of planning into the Christmas programme. Something like this is bound to put a bit of a damper on proceedings."

Jack didn't comment on the understatement. Instead, implacably he pronounced, "This is a suspicious death. In cases of suspicious death, the police have to be informed."

"Yes. Right. Well, I'd better lock the chapel up and get on the telephone."

Maria looked expectantly at Jack. Surely he wasn't going to leave the scene of the crime so quickly? He would want to make a more thorough examination, bring his old skills to bear, glean some more clues from the murder location.

But his eyes gave her a little negative flick, which she immediately understood. He was telling her that everyone, even Roddy Stout, was at that moment a suspect. The word "murder" hadn't yet been mentioned in Roddy's hearing – safer to keep it that way for the time being.

Jack gave a long look at the back of the Puzzel shield, memorising its details, then turned his wheelchair to leave the chapel. Maria walked meekly beside him.

They were at the door when Roddy Stout's voice stopped them. "I would very much appreciate it if you didn't mention this unfortunate incident to any of the other guests."

"It'll have to come out sooner or later. They're going to notice once the police arrive and start questioning them."

"Yes, I appreciate that, Mr Tarrant, but could we make it later rather than sooner? Let's keep the thing quiet as long as we can. Get as far into the Christmas Break as possible before it all falls apart." A new pleading note had come into his voice. "At least let's not spoil the Ice-breaking Reception. That's due to start in half an hour."

Jack Tarrant nodded curtly. "All right. We won't say anything . . . so long as you guarantee that you get straight on to the police."

"Of course. You can rely on me."

The Reception Desk was unattended as they passed. On the counter lay the plushly upholstered Visitors' Book. It was typical of the Puzzel Manor Country House style of presentation that this form of registration should be used, rather than a modern computerised card system.

"Quick, Maria," said Jack. "Use the photocopier and copy the relevant pages."

She needed no second bidding and was immediately behind the counter. "Want your list of suspects, do you?"

He nodded grimly. "And pass me the telephone. I've still got friends in the West Midlands Constabulary, and I'm not sure that I trust Mr Roddy Stout to get across the full urgency of the situation."

She passed a phone down to him and turned to the photocopier. Jack Tarrant looked with satisfaction at the number on the dial as he picked up the receiver. But then his expression changed.

"Damn. It's dead."

Maria, hearing a sound from the office behind, seemingly in one movement replaced the Visitors' Book, secreted the photocopy up her sleeve to join the dead vicar's notebook, and moved to the other side of the counter. She looked up innocently at the girl who emerged through the office door.

It was the one who had welcomed them earlier, still identified by the lapel badge on her neat blue suit as "NERYS – Assistant Manager". She was compact, with luxuriantly long black hair and pert dark eyes.

"Hello," she said brightly. Then, seeing the telephone on Jack's lap, pointed out, "You do have a telephone in your room, you know, sir."

"Don't think it'd be much more use to me than this one," said Jack, holding the receiver towards her. "Nothing."

Nerys took the instrument and listened for a moment to its

16

total silence. "Oh no!" she wailed. "The snow must have brought the lines down. That's all we need!"

"Why? Other things been going wrong?" asked Maria casually.

The girl, embarrassed by her momentary lapse into emotion, was quickly back into efficient executive mode. "Well, the weather certainly hasn't made things easy for us. The two girls who were going to come up from Puzzel Moultby and help over this Christmas Break phoned half an hour ago. The drifts are so deep they can't get through."

"Oh dear."

"Which only means that I'll end up having to act as waitress and chambermaid and washer-upper, which was not what I trained at college for, and . . ." She realised she was letting her guests see rather too much of the Puzzel Manor stage-management and again recovered herself. "Oh, well, never mind. Can't be helped. Let's just hope we don't get any power cuts to add to our problems. That would be the absolute last straw!"

"Don't you have a generator?"

"It's been installed, sir, but not connected up. The electrician was coming this morning but, because of the weather . . ." She shrugged and spread her hands helplessly. "But don't worry, sir and madam, we will not allow anything to spoil your enjoyment of the Christmas Break."

Not even a murder? thought both Jack and Maria.

"Convenient for Roddy Stout, isn't it?" said Jack when they were back in the Yellow Room. He was riffling hurriedly through the contents of his briefcase for a sheet of paper.

"What do you mean?"

"Phones going down. Means he can't contact the police. Means, so long as we keep our mouths shut, his precious Christmas Break will not be interrupted by the ugly spectre of murder."

His pencil moved deftly over the blank sheet, drawing out a series of criss-crossed lines.

"Jack, are you saying he might have cut off the phone lines deliberately?"

"He'd have been hard pushed to do it in time . . . unless of course he already knew what he was going to find in the chapel."

"You think that's possible?"

"In this situation, Maria, anything's possible. What's the time?"

"Five to six."

"Got to hurry. I want to be there right at the beginning of this Ice-breaking Reception – see them all as they come in."

Maria studied the photocopy of the Visitors' Book. "Twelve guests, including us. Reckon it must be one of them?"

"Someone who's on the premises, certainly. But don't forget the staff," he said as he continued to draw. "That means Roddy Stout, Jan Stout, Nerys, the chef – Anders Whateverhisname is . . . and maybe others we don't know about. There."

He finished the drawing with a flourish. Maria looked over his shoulder.

"Is that what was marked on the back of the shield?"

"Yes, a kind of grid."

"What do you reckon it's for?"

"I reckon this is the board on which the murderer wants us to play his evil game."

"What, but –"

"No time to explain now. We must get to this reception."

"We haven't looked at the dead man's notebook yet."

"That'll have to wait, too. Come on. Just show me the page from the Visitors' Book. I want to know who I'm up against."

Maria handed across the sheet, which Jack Tarrant studied for a moment of intense concentration, committing its details to his memory.

The Ice-breaking Reception did not get the Christmas Break off to a good start. Indeed, in its early stages, Jack and Maria found themselves wondering whether a public announcement about the body in the chapel might not have made for a better social atmosphere.

The trouble was that, rather than just letting time and alcohol perform their customary slow erosion of British reserve, Roddy and Jan Stout had decided that what was really needed to get things going was a "game". Now, that kind of thing might work well with Americans or races of a more outgoing, participatory

DATE	NAME	ADDRESS
19/12/91	Bob and Barbara Hood	1712, Sherman Drive, Woodland Hills, CA 91364 US
20/12/91	_(illegible)_	
21st December	Lady Drakeridge	14B _(illegible)_ W2
"	Trudy Bastable	4A Medina Mansions, London NW8.
22/12/91	Count Leo Leontchy	"
23/12/91	Peggy Smith-Brously	—
24th	Celia Tranmere	High Ridges, Plakiston Avenue, Cheltenham 23C Horbury Sq. W11 3NT
"	Col. Honeycutt	Aldershot
"	Alexander Honeycutt	14 Leatham Lane, Camberley, Surrey
"	Jack Tarrant	34 Juniper Road, Richmond, Surrey
"	Maria Lethbury	"

nature, but it has always been hopeless in England. There is nothing so calculated to increase the height of the walls of reticence with which the British surround themselves as coercing them into undignified activity.

Roddy and Jan Stout (a blonded, hard-faced woman whose elaborate vowels suggested her husband might have married a little beneath himself) were present in the south drawing room, plying their guests with champagne and nibbles, but the actual game was organised by an avuncular gentleman in his sixties. He introduced himself as Trentham Metcalfe (clearly the inscriber of the second, illegible signature in the Visitors' Book), who had been employed by the Stouts to act as "Master of the Revels" over the Christmas Break. He then undertook to explain the "very simple" rules of the game they were about to play.

The trouble, of course, was that the rules were far from simple. Trentham Metcalfe didn't seem to have a very good grasp of them himself, and an occasional slurring of his words, together with a certain wildness in his eyes, suggested that alcohol might have contributed to his confusion.

He was a plump man, clearly an actor from his fruity delivery and the histrionic manner in which he repeatedly swept back his mane of white hair. Anyone getting within a metre of his breath could readily identify his enthusiasm for whisky.

What would happen, he explained eagerly, was that each person present would have a label with a name and profession pinned on to his or her back, and then they all had to ask questions of the other guests to find out who they were and what they did.

"Couldn't be simpler. And won't it be *fun?*" he asked of the stony-faced circle of armchairs in the south drawing room.

"Why do we do this? You haven't explained what possible purpose will be served by our going through this grotesque masquerade?" asked a chillingly precise upper-class voice.

It belonged to Lady Deathridge, a septuagenarian who resembled some tiny bird with a vindictive peck. Trudy Bastable, her companion, plump forty and with the looks of someone who'd never stirred a flicker in a male heart, leant across and hissed, "Be quiet, Annabelle."

"Well, er . . ." Trentham Metcalfe floundered, trying to

provide an answer to Lady Deathridge's question.

He was saved the trouble by Peggy Smith-Brously, substantial and sixty, spilling out of a dress whose extremely highly paid designer had visualised it on someone just about to enter their twenties. "It's perfectly obvious. We play this game to get a convivial atmosphere going."

"Can't wait for that, love," drawled Celia Tranmere. She could, with charity and a bit of imagination, be placed on the right side of fifty, and her demeanour placed her as firmly as Trentham Metcalfe within the theatrical profession.

The actor looked rather nervously at his employer, but wasn't getting any help there. Roddy Stout deliberately avoided Trentham's eye, though by doing so he caught the eye of Jack Tarrant. The hotelier gave a competent, don't-worry-everything-in-hand kind of nod.

"I think it sounds terrific fun," announced Alexander Honeycutt, who, at thirteen, was by some fifteen years the youngest person in the room. He sat by his father, a reduced facsimile in almost identical navy blazer, grey trousers and black brogues.

Jack and Maria had made a deduction from the different addresses in the Visitors' Book that Alexander lived with his divorced mother and that it was his father's turn to have the boy for Christmas. They had the feeling there might be other products of domestic disharmony present at Puzzel Manor. It's not usually the people in satisfactory relationships who seek out the anonymity of an hotel for Christmas.

"I don't know. Don't approve of play-acting. Turns boys into nancies," said Colonel Honeycutt gruffly. He was probably in his late forties, but had that seasoned-timber fitness that would keep him looking the same for another twenty years.

"Oh, well, I think it's just a great idea," Bob Hood enthused warmly. "Barbara and I had heard you British like playing games at Christmastime, and all we want to do is play right along with you."

"That's right, Bob," his wife agreed.

Trentham Metcalfe seized the lifeline greedily. "Terrific! Come on – who's going to be the first to have their label pinned on?"

21

"I am very happy for it to be me." The voice was beautifully cultured, only its deepness and precision suggesting any foreign origin. The rest of Count Leo Leontchy was also beautifully cultured, from his neatly set hair to his pearl cuff-links and manicured nails. He was short, and plumpish, with a grey goatee beard and monocle on a black silk ribbon.

He meekly turned his back to Trentham Metcalfe, and the actor, after consulting a list, pinned a label on to the back of the immaculate suit. It read "RONALD STEDSMAN – Film Actor".

In spite of his father's evident disapproval, Alexander Honeycutt was the next to leap forward. He returned as "DALE N. SANDSTORM – US Army General".

Bob and Barbara Hood hurried keenly up to have their labels attached, and left as "SAM LADD-TRENSON – Arctic Explorer" and "TESS NORMANDAL – Swedish Film Star" respectively.

Peggy Smith-Brously was labelled "SANDRA S. DELMONT – American Romantic Novelist", Celia Tranmere was transformed into "DR. ÖSTLANDESMAN – Psychiatrist", and Trudy Bastable had "MS. LORNA DESTAND – Feminist Academic" pinned on her back.

Jack and Maria had no desire to be standoffish and they submitted to being tagged as "DONALD N. MASTERS – American Film Producer" and "DAME D.L.S. TRANSON – Crimewriter".

Only Lady Deathridge and Colonel Honeycutt resolutely refused to join in, so the labels reading "DENSTON SMALARD – Racing Driver" and "MRS. ANN SEAL-TODD – Show-jumper" went unclaimed.

Although he had persuaded most of the potential participants to participate, Trentham Metcalfe could not really have claimed that the game was a success. Only the Hoods and Alexander Honeycutt really entered into the spirit of the thing. Celia Tranmere started with great enthusiasm, swooping operatically on people and forcing them to answer her questions, but she soon tired and went to sit down. There she emptied her champagne glass with a frequency only matched by the speed with which Jan Stout kept filling it up again.

22

Some ice-breaking did take place during the reception, but the general view was that the same effect would have been less painfully achieved by forgetting the game entirely, and leaving the champagne to work its own quiet miracle. All in all, there was considerable relief when Roddy Stout announced that supper would be in the dining room in fifteen minutes, and that anyone who wanted to go and freshen up should take the opportunity to do so.

The room emptied with what, to him as organiser of the Christmas Break, must have been rather dispiriting speed.

Maria Lethbury noticed that Trentham Metcalfe had been one of the first to leave, and concluded that he had rushed back to the embottled source of that which so heavily flavoured his breath. He hadn't taken the list of the guests and their labelled identities with him, so she casually picked it up.

She had a feeling that all kinds of scraps of paper might be relevant over the ensuing forty-eight hours.

In the Yellow Room, Jack Tarrant explained to her the drawing he had made earlier. "You see, the back of the shield is divided into sections, like so, and . . ." he picked up the "With Compliments" slip which had held the first puzzle – "this strange motif in the bottom right-hand corner is –"

"Part of the Puzzel coat of arms." Maria Lethbury, never accused of being slow on the uptake, completed the sentence for him.

"Exactly. Now, given what the answer to the first puzzle was – and the fact that when you reverse the coat of arms, that word has to fit in the top left-hand corner – I think when we have filled in the whole shield, we will find that we have a message from the murderer."

"How many squares are there?"

"Nineteen."

Maria whistled. "So we've got to solve nineteen puzzles?"

"Possibly. The solutions to some may go over more than one square. We don't know that yet. It'll make our job easier if I number the squares, though." He picked up a pencil and matched his actions to his words. "And, of course, I hope we catch the villain before he gets a chance to tease us with *all* of his puzzles."

Maria slumped thoughtfully into an armchair, and then remembered the notebook she had taken from the murder victim's pocket. "Maybe we'll find another puzzle in here."

"Wouldn't surprise me," Jack agreed gloomily. "There, done the numbering. Now . . ." He picked up a Puzzel Manor brochure with the family coat of arms on the front and started ruling lines on it. "This'll make it easier to identify which square on the back corresponds to which piece of the coat of arms."

"God, it's impossible to imagine the sort of mind that would do all this, isn't it, Jack?"

"Not completely impossible, I hope. We've got to try and get *inside* this monster's mind. Only by thinking as he thinks can we hope to catch him – and to stop further murders."

"Right." Maria returned her attention to the notebook. "This all seems to be just notes for sermons, that kind of thing . . ."

"Keep looking," said Jack.

He finished his diagrams and then filled in the answer to the first puzzle.

"Ah, there's something here," Maria announced.

She moved across to Jack and showed him the open page of the notebook.

"Yes, there's the piece of the coat of arms all right." He consulted his diagrams. "And the solution to the second puzzle will fit right next door to the first one." He looked back at the handwritten pages. "Well, they're all biblical texts . . . ideas for sermons, presumably?"

"I imagine so." Maria Lethbury's brow furrowed. She wasn't a bishop's daughter for nothing. "No, they're not *all* biblical texts . . ."

"The false one's the puzzle?"

"Right." She pointed to the page. "And I'll lay you any money that that's the one . . ."

"Hm, but –"

"Oh no!" Maria breathed in horror. "'Starting Points' . . ."

And, as she wrote the solution to the second Puzzel Manor puzzle in its rightful square, her lover turned very pale.

24

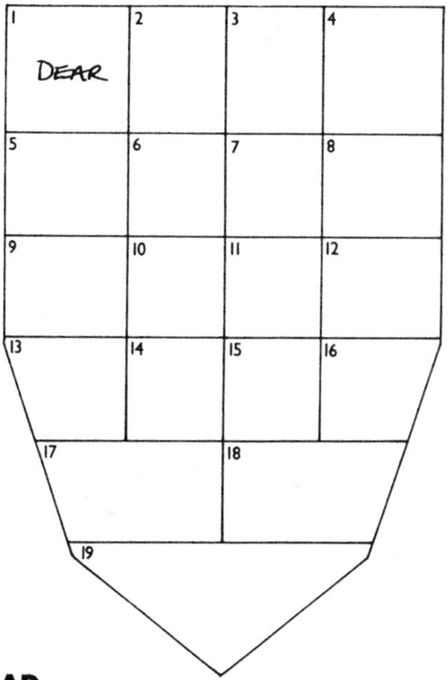

THIS IS HOW JACK TARRANT HAD WORKED OUT THE FIRST PUZZLE:

He noticed that the telephone number on the "With Compliments" slip did not correspond with the one on the original Puzzel Manor Christmas Break brochure. From the way that the numbers of the false phone number were laid out, he deduced that they must correspond to letters appearing somewhere else on the slip. The only sequence of words where they made any sense was the motto beneath the coat of arms (also different from its appearance on the brochure). By counting the letters from the beginning of the motto, Jack Tarrant found the solution as entered on the shield.

STARTING POINTS ?

In the morning sow thy seed,
and in the evening withhold
not thine hand

       (Ecclesiastes 11)

A fool uttereth all his mind.

       (Proverbs 29)

We should also walk in
newness of life .

       (Romans 6)

Justice and charity, knoweth
the Almighty, reward righteous
acolytes

       (Nahum 2)

And in mercy shall the
throne be established

       (Isaiah 16)

Jeshurun waxed fat,
and kicked.

       (Deuteronomy 32)

THREE

CHRISTMAS EVE –
10.00 P.M. GHOST STORY

The supper was delicious. Though the guests had been given assurances that the main Christmas meals would be punctiliously English and traditional, for that evening Anders Altmidson had been allowed to indulge his native skills. So they ate lavishly garnished Scandinavian pork with an imaginative selection of vegetables, followed by a range of delicate fruit confections and pastries.

The Puzzel Manor cellar proved to be well stocked and its wines, on top of the champagne already consumed, made the atmosphere convivial – or at least as convivial as English people on their first day of meeting ever allow their atmospheres to get.

Those who had arrived only that day were relieved to discover how good the food was. Forty-eight hours of such eating was a most appealing prospect.

The dishes were attractively presented – Anders Altmidson was aware that presentation counted for at least as much as taste in contemporary cuisine – and affably served by the Stouts and Nerys. If she still nursed resentment at having to take on duties beneath the dignity of an Assistant Manager, she was professional enough to keep it to herself.

Jack Tarrant and Maria Lethbury enjoyed their meal, and took the opportunity for a little surreptitious questioning of the other guests at their table, building up a store of information to pool and

27

discuss when they were next alone together. In spite of the conviviality, though, neither of them could forget the evidence of murder they had witnessed in the chapel. Nor the fact that the murderer had embroiled them personally in his vicious game-playing.

At the end of the meal Roddy Stout announced that coffee and liqueurs would be served in the south drawing room, and that he hoped all guests would assemble by the large fire in the hotel's entrance hall at ten o'clock for a spine-chilling Ghost Story.

Jack Tarrant made sure that he and Maria were the last to leave the dining room, and cornered the proprietor by the door. "Why didn't you make an announcement about the fact that there won't be a Midnight Mass?" he demanded sharply.

Roddy Stout looked uncomfortable. "I thought I'd tell them after the Ghost Story . . . give them less time to worry about it or speculate on the reasons for the cancellation."

"Hm. Have you managed to get through to the police?"

The hotelier shrugged apologetically. "Phone lines are down."

"Surely you must have some other means of making contact? This is an emergency. Haven't you got a carphone?" Roddy Stout shook his head. "Well, have you asked whether any of the guests have carphones? Colonel Honeycutt was saying he drove through the drifts in his Range Rover – he's just the type to have his vehicle fully equipped with everything. Have you asked him?"

"No. Carphones don't work out here, anyway. Too far from any aerials for the signal to carry."

"Well, there must be some other way of making contact. Can't someone go to the nearest house and try using their phone?"

"Nearest house is the vicarage – and there won't be anyone there, will there? Anyway, it's still snowing. It's impossible even to get out of the house in this weather."

"Doesn't strike me you've tried too hard to get out," Maria observed.

"I haven't had a lot of time!" Roddy Stout sounded aggrieved. "I am trying to run an hotel here, you know."

"And part of running an hotel," said Jack Tarrant drily, "is reporting deaths on your premises to the proper authorities."

28

"I've tried!" said the proprietor with an unsuccessful attempt at assertiveness.

"Well, at least I trust you've kept the chapel locked and haven't touched the body?"

"Well, erm . . ."

Roddy Stout looked so uncomfortable that his interrogator knew the truth instantly. "For God's sake, where have you put it?"

"There's an old ice-house just outside the kitchen door," the proprietor mumbled. "I've put it in there."

Jack Tarrant was almost beside himself. "You fool! Surely you know you shouldn't tamper with the evidence in a case like this!"

"What do you mean – a case like this? What we have here is just an unfortunate accident. It'd be different if we were talking about a murder."

He sounded totally convincing, as if he believed in what he was saying. But that fact didn't really help the two investigators much. If Roddy Stout was the murderer, he would make it his business to sound totally convincing.

"Don't worry about it," said Jack.

They were back in the Yellow Room. His wheelchair was by the window, and he opened the striped curtains a crack to see the snow that still fell relentlessly.

"But, Jack, if he's moved the body, then any evidence in the chapel will have been destroyed."

"Yes, but we got a good look at the scene. I'm pretty clear what happened. And if we do need to examine the body, at least we know where to find it."

Maria nodded. "In the ice-house. Do you think Roddy Stout is really as innocent as he appears?"

"My instinct is to say yes. I don't think he moved the body deliberately to tamper with the evidence. I think he's just trying to salvage his precious Christmas Break. Must've put a lot of money into doing this place up. He knows that murder's bad for business and so he wants the whole affair hushed up for as long as possible."

"Yes." Maria Lethbury rubbed her chin reflectively. "You

29

know, there were a couple of things that struck me about the body in the chapel . . ."

"Me too. Tell me yours first."

"All right. As you know, given how I was brought up, I've met quite a lot of clergymen in my time . . ."

"Of course."

"And the Church is not a profession from which, under normal circumstances, people retire early. My father the bishop is nearly seventy and he shows no signs of giving it up. He's got as much energy as ever he had."

Jack Tarrant grinned. "I think your mother the actress may have something to do with that."

"Perhaps. Be that as it may, what I'm saying is that the man we saw dead in the chapel looked far too young to be retired – or even semi-retired – from the Church."

"I'd had the same thought."

"And the jottings in his notebook looked too contrived, too schematised. All right, I know the 'Starting Points' thing was part of a puzzle, but none of the rest of the notes looked right either. No vicar I've ever met has written out notes like that."

"No. What is more – his dog-collar and bib were both absolutely brand-new."

"I think we're both saying the same thing, Jack – that, whoever the murder victim may have been, he wasn't the Rev. Verdure."

"No. Which of course raises the fascinating question – who was he and what was he doing in the Puzzel Manor chapel?" Jack Tarrant was lost in thought for a moment. "We've got to find out more about everyone in this house. So far we have only the sketchiest of information."

"I think their dates of arrival may be significant," said Maria. "We can check those in the Visitors' Book. I mean, setting this whole thing up was bound to take a lot of preparation. So, for instance, it's unlikely that we should be looking for Colonel Honeycutt as our murderer, because he and Alexander only made it here this afternoon."

"You're probably right, but we can't rule anything out yet." Jack looked fretfully at his drawing of the shield grid with its two completed squares. "This is just so horribly personal. It's directed straight at me. The murderer is challenging *me*."

Maria put her hand on his shoulder. "Don't worry. You'll be equal to that challenge."

"Hm." A grim new thought struck him. "Oh no!"

"What?"

"I've suddenly realised how completely we were set up. The murderer's orchestrated this whole bloody thing just to humiliate me."

"How do you mean?"

He pointed to his name in its square inside the shield shape. "Initial letters, Maria. No wonder we'd never heard of the Police Injuries Subscription Society."

She worked it out for herself and groaned. "And to think I encouraged you to come."

"Played straight into the murderer's hands. Oh, he or she's taking the 'piss' all right."

For a moment he looked defeated, his will wavering, but he quickly regained control. His next words were very positive. "But he's not going to defeat me. Look, I want to search the bedrooms of the rest of the guests. Whoever's set all this up is going to have a store of paper and writing implements, at the very least. If I can find those –"

"But, Jack, how're you going to manage to do that?"

"There's a lift, isn't there?" He sounded defensive, as if she were again drawing attention to his disability. "And I'm pretty mobile in this thing."

"I don't mean that. I mean how're you going to get into the bedrooms when there's nobody around?"

"During one of the scheduled events." He looked at his watch. "I'll have a go while this Ghost Story's on. You go and listen and make some excuse for my absence."

"Yes, of course I will." She hesitated. "You don't think it'd be simpler if I searched the bedrooms and –"

Unfortunately he took this as another criticism of his mobility. "No. I will do it. I've more experience than you have of searching premises. I –"

He was stopped by the sudden extinction of all the lights in the

31

room. They were left with only the feeble glow of the untended fire.

Maria moved quickly to open the door. The corridor too was dark. "Power cut."

"Damn!"

"It's all right, Jack. I'm sure the hotel's got plenty of candles and –"

"I wasn't thinking of light. I was thinking of the lift."

"Oh." She realised the full implication of his words.

He grinned at her wryly through the half-light. "So I'm not going to be able to do my search upstairs, am I, love?"

"I'm sorry. It's just –"

"No. You do it for me, Maria. You know I trust you."

"Yes, but –"

"I was always being told at Scotland Yard that I wasn't much good at delegating. Now it's forced on me. Would you mind being my eyes and legs, Maria?"

"I'd be honoured. What are you going to do?"

"Me? Oh, I think I'd better listen to the Ghost Story."

"'. . . but when Sir Henry Puzzel brought his young bride to Puzzel Manor from the continent in 1857, no one realised that she was suffering from a severe form of inherited mental illness.

"'They had met earlier that year at the fashionable spa of Baden Baden, and fallen instantly in love.

"'Sonia told Sir Henry that she had no family, and indeed that was true. What she did not tell him – and it is quite possible that she had erased the fact from her mind – was that she had been responsible for the deaths of her mother and father. Both of them she had strangled at the family home in Randers.

"'After these dreadful crimes, Sonia had been committed to a secure institution, whence, using the exceptional cunning which characterised her particular form of insanity, she had managed to escape. What she did from that moment till she resurfaced with a new identity some four years later in Baden Baden, no one has ever been able to find out. And indeed those details of her early life that are known only came to light after her tragic death.'"

Trentham Metcalfe let the pause linger in the dim, candlelit air, confident of the hypnotic effect of his practised voice. His audience did indeed seem mesmerised, gathered in a circle round the huge sighing logs of the open fireplace, whose orange flames had long given way to a deep pink glow. More soft light spilled from the guarded candles on the tall, glittering Christmas tree that stood, surrounded by shinily wrapped presents, at the foot of the stairs.

Trentham was an old ham and had had more recourse to the whisky bottle since supper, but professional instinct and the intensity of the story he was telling guaranteed his performance.

He read from an old leatherbound volume, whose pages were covered with spidery handwriting. The book appeared to be a history of the Puzzel family, and Jack Tarrant was determined that, if he got the opportunity once the Ghost Story was finished, he would look through it.

He glanced round the rapt assembly with satisfaction. The only absentees were Jan Stout, Nerys, the chef whom nobody had yet met, and Maria Lethbury, for whose sudden attack of migraine Jack had apologised. The fireside circle in the entrance hall included all the other guests, none of them aware of Maria above them, deftly and silently flashing her pencil torch through their belongings.

Jack Tarrant looked across at Roddy Stout. There had still been no announcement about the cancellation of the Midnight Mass, but the proprietor appeared totally caught up in the Ghost Story, which seemed to be as new to him as it was to any of his guests.

"'At first . . .'" Trentham Metcalfe rolled the "r" heavily as he picked up his narrative – "'all seemed well with the newly-weds. Local resistance to having a foreigner as mistress of Puzzel Manor quickly receded as the villagers of Puzzel Moultby came to appreciate Sonia's beauty and good nature and, when it was made public, the news of her pregnancy was universally welcomed.

"'It was only after the birth of Gervaise Puzzel that the latent madness in his mother reasserted itself. The arrival of a boy child, a male heir to Puzzel Manor, had been greeted with great rejoicing. Gervaise was born on Christmas Day, and superstitious local folk attributed some kind of magic to this fact, as if the newborn baby would indeed be a saviour, a talisman which – like the famous Puzzel shield – would protect the family and its dependants for years to come.

"'Sir Henry was ecstatic with joy; Sonia appeared to be a tender and loving mother; and Gervaise Puzzel, according to the testimony of the local doctor, was a robust and perfect baby.

"'It was a hard winter into which the child had been born. Snow had blanketed the Cotswolds for most of the month of December, and showed no signs of shifting as Christmas gave way to the New Year.

"'And it was into that cruel snow that, suddenly and for no apparent reason, Sonia Puzzel took her week-old baby . . . and abandoned him.

"'She left him, early in the morning of New Year's Eve, under the yew tree that still stands by the main gates of Puzzel Manor. Then she returned to the house, and started to play the piano, blithe, unconcerned, as if nothing had happened. And, indeed, it is possible that she had no recollection of what she had done, that she had blacked out her crime, just as she had blacked out the murder of her parents.

"'It was some hours before the household realised that the child was missing. When the nursery nurse asked after her charge, Sonia Puzzel smilingly told her that he was sleeping. It was nearly dark by the time anxiety as to the baby's whereabouts developed. His mother could not give – or was unwilling to give – any clue as to where he might be found.

"'A search of the estate was hastily instituted, and within half an hour Gervaise Puzzel was found. By then, the baby, dressed only in a thin gown and blanket, had been exposed to the Arctic conditions for nearly ten hours.

"'Miraculously, he lived through the ordeal. But it would be wrong to say that he survived unscathed. The blaze of the surrounding snow on his young eyes had left Gervaise Puzzel permanently blind.

"'And, as he grew up, it was clear that his mind too had been scarred. Perhaps he would have inherited his mother's illness

34

anyway, but the ordeal in the snow brought a bizarre variation to his particular form of insanity. Though always highly strung, the boy became uncontrollably mad only when snow fell. Although unable to see the snow, he could sense it, and it triggered in him an illness at least as cunning and as homicidal as his mother's.

"'Sir Henry Puzzel lived out his life in mounting despair. At first unable to believe his wife's actions, he blamed the nurse, who was summarily dismissed, and tried to continue as if nothing had happened. After a year his wife became pregnant again and gave birth to a daughter.

"'That child she strangled when it was one week old.

"'And, since the infanticide had been witnessed by a young housemaid, from that moment there was no pretending that Sonia Puzzel was normal.

"'Sir Henry managed, by bribing the housemaid and by local influence, to keep this crime from the authorities, and devoted the rest of his life to guarding his mad wife and his blind son, in whose behaviour madness became daily more apparent.

"'Poor man – how he suffered! The atmosphere in Puzzel Manor must have threatened his own sanity. The house was full of the sounds of his wife's manic piano-playing and the tap-tap-tapping of his sightless son's stick. And all the time Sir Henry Puzzel watched and waited, never certain when the fits of madness would be visited on them.

"'The end came suddenly. Gervaise was nearing his nine-teenth birthday. Christmas was approaching and once again the snow fell. The young man, as always when it snowed, was locked up in his room, but on that Christmas Eve, Sonia Puzzel managed to escape her husband's vigilance for long enough to break out of the house. She left Sir Henry a note, saying she could stand her mental torment no longer. She was determined to end it all at the bottom of the lake in the grounds of Puzzel Manor.

"'They found her shawl by the lakeside. They saw the hole where the ice had broken. But though, when the thaw came, they dragged the lake, her body was never found.

"'Gervaise survived his mother by exactly one year. The following Christmas, Puzzel Manor was once again blanketed with snow. On Christmas Eve, the day before his twentieth birthday, the blind youth cunningly unpicked the lock on his bedroom door. He left a note saying, "I have gone to join my mother."

"'He left the house at the same time his mother had the year before, and he must somehow have made his sightless way to the lake.

"'They found his overcoat by the lakeside. They saw the hole where the ice had broken. But, though the lake was later dragged, his body, like his mother's, stayed down, trapped forever in the murky depths.

"'Sir Henry, the last of the Puzzels, died within the year, a broken man.'"

The actor dropped his voice thrillingly low, as he reached the climax of his story.

"'But they say that, though Gervaise Puzzel's body is dead, his mad, anguished spirit can find no rest.

"'They say that, when snow falls at Christmastime, blind Gervaise Puzzel still walks round Puzzel Manor.

"'And they say that, in the stillness of the night, the tap-tap-tap of his stick can – still – be – heard.'"

The last words, long and separate, were as soft as breath. There was a total silence.

Then suddenly came the sound of tapping from behind them, near the front door.

Celia Tranmere screamed.

It was the Rev. Verdure.

A hearty, wizened man in his seventies, who had been a keen skier in his time, he had donned cross-country skis and made his way across from the vicarage.

Thus proving incontrovertibly what Jack Tarrant had never doubted – that the body in the chapel at Puzzel Manor belonged to someone else.

Not trusting Roddy Stout to do it, Jack immediately asked the vicar if his telephone was working. The answer was negative. The Rev. Verdure was of the opinion that all the lines in Puzzel Moultby and the surrounding area were down. He then briskly asked Roddy Stout for directions to the chapel, so that he could prepare for his service.

This was a signal for the assembly to break up. Some went upstairs to bed, others to get ready for the Midnight Mass. One or two wandered to the Hunters' Bar off the hall for a drink. As they all left, Jack was delighted to see that Trentham Metcalfe had left the leatherbound book on his armchair. The detective picked it up and flicked through the pages.

As he'd suspected, it was a hand-written history of the Puzzel family. It had no formal structure; entries had been added at different times in different hands. Some were sustained pieces of writing like the Ghost Story, others little more than notes, the kind of basic details of births and deaths that might be entered into a family Bible.

Jack Tarrant found what he was looking for towards the end of the book. It was the last page on which anything had been written. The writing was thin and formal, the hand of a Victorian clerk, but a design in the bottom right-hand corner left Jack Tarrant in no doubt that its origins were more recent.

He felt a hand on his shoulder. "Any luck?" he asked without looking round.

"Not a lot," said Maria. "You?"

"Something here." He pointed to the writing on the page in front of him. "Haven't quite worked it out yet, though."

"Well, Concarneau's not in Normandy, for a start. It's in Brittany."

"Yes, but –"

"Oh, come on, Jack, that one's *easy*," said Maria Lethbury.

37

The End of the Line

Sir Gervaise Poucelle came to England in 1066 from the little Norman town of Concarneau. His descendant Sir Henry Puzzel built Puzzel Manor and for many years his heirs owned the land, until the unfortunate madness of another Gervaise meant that the Puzzel estates passed to a new owner.

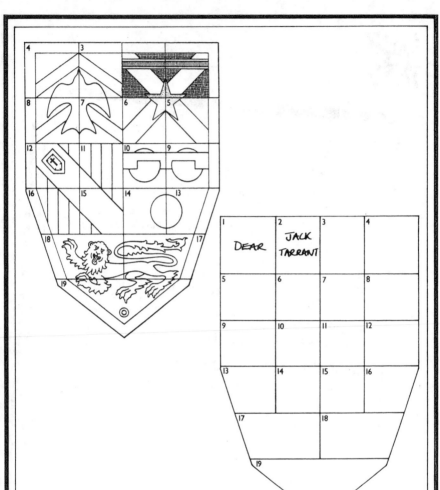

1 DEAR	2 JACK TARRANT	3	4
5	6	7	8
9	10	11	12
13	14	15	16
17		18	
19			

THIS IS HOW MARIA LETHBURY HAD WORKED OUT THE SECOND PUZZLE:

Recognising the rogue quotation to be the fourth one, and taking a clue from the heading of the page, "STARTING POINTS", Maria took the initial letters of the quotation in sequence. So it read: "<u>J</u>ustice <u>a</u>nd <u>c</u>harity, <u>k</u>noweth <u>t</u>he <u>A</u>lmighty, <u>r</u>eward <u>r</u>ighteous <u>a</u>colytes". (<u>N</u>ahum 2 - i.e. <u>t</u>wo)

FOUR

CHRISTMAS EVE –
11.30 P.M. MIDNIGHT
MASS IN THE
PUZZEL CHAPEL

J ack Tarrant had a copy of his shield grid with him and filled in
the word in the relevant square. His mouth was set in a grim
line. Idly, hardly noticing what he looked at, he turned the pages
of the leatherbound book on his lap while Maria brought him up to
date on her exploration upstairs.

"I didn't find anything that was definitely incriminating. One or
two things that were quite interesting, mind . . ."

"Like what?"

"Like, for instance, the fact that Colonel Honeycutt has a pistol
and ammunition in his luggage, along with a coil of climbing ropes
with clips, and a fairly nasty-looking hunting knife."

"Hm, that might be significant. On the other hand, he is exactly
the type who would carry that sort of stuff around. Macho, self-
sufficiency image seems pretty important to him."

"Yes. We should find out what branch of the army he's in –
might be important."

"I'd put money on the SAS. Or at least that he's SAS-trained.

Whether he's still in it now, I wouldn't know. Any other potential murder weapons?"

"Well – surprise, surprise – Trentham Metcalfe's got enough Scotch in his room to kill someone."

"Ha, ha," said Jack drily.

"Otherwise, Alexander Honeycutt's got a Swiss Army knife . . ."

"Predictable. I bet it was a present from his father."

"Mm. Though the boy seems more interested in artistic than active pursuits. He's brought a lot of paints and pencils with him, calligraphic pens and so on . . ."

"Which is just the kind of stuff whoever's setting all these puzzles is going to need."

"Yes . . ." The bishop and actress's daughter looked dubious. "Can we really put a thirteen-year-old boy on our list of suspects?"

"At the moment I don't think we can exclude any possibility – however outrageous."

"No. Right."

"Anything else?"

"From the equipment he carries around with him, it seems that Count Leo Leontchy has something of a cocaine habit."

"Ah."

"Whether that's significant or not, I don't know."

"Depends on who else knows about it. I mean, if someone wanted to blackmail him . . . well, it might be useful. Find out any other nasty secrets?"

"Well, Peggy Smith-Brously's got an extremely convenient set of murder weapons in her room. The question is whether she knows she has."

"Don't *you* start setting puzzles, Maria. I've got quite enough on my plate with the murderer."

"All right. It's just that she's brought all her Christmas presents along with her – I mean the ones that she's been given, and she hasn't opened any of them yet . . ."

"You, however, have opened them?"

"Yes, and done them up again perfectly – don't worry, she'll never know they've been touched. Anyway, among her gifts is a very swish set of stainless steel kitchen knives."

"Who from?"

"A son. Called Melvyn. Very formal little gift tag. 'Happy Christmas, Mother. From Melvyn.'"

"No 'Love'?"

"No. No 'Love' – which may or may not be significant. Could be a very Freudian gesture – a son giving his mother a set of knives – particularly a son whose mother has to spend Christmas on her own in an hotel . . ."

"On the other hand, it could just mean that he's a sensitive and observant lad, and when he was last in his mother's kitchen he noticed she needed some new knives . . ."

"Yes – or, if one goes for the ultimately devious scenario, it could be an easy way for Peggy Smith-Brously to smuggle in a murder weapon . . ."

"It could indeed. What else did you find?"

"Well, old Lady Deathridge's practically got a portable chemist shop with her. Plenty of sleeping pills, that kind of stuff, which are all potentially murderous, I suppose."

"What about her companion? Are they sharing a room, by the way?"

"No, Trudy Bastable's got her own room next door. Not as lavish as Lady Deathridge's, but all right."

"Anything in it?"

"Hardly a thing. It's strange. I've never seen anyone with so little luggage. One change of clothes, toothbrush – that's about it."

"So, if nobody's actually sharing a room, it must mean –"

"Alexander Honeycutt's sharing with his father."

"Ah. No doubt so that the Colonel can keep the heating turned down and ensure the boy does a hundred press-ups before breakfast. Poor little sod."

"However," Maria announced slyly, "I think there's someone else who's *planning* to share a room . . ." Jack cocked a quizzical eye at her. "I found a letter in Celia Tranmere's suitcase. A love letter. Pretty steamy one, actually . . . detailing all the things someone is proposing to do to her 'when we're alone together at Puzzel Manor over Christmas'."

43

"Really? Any clue as to his identity?"

Maria shook her head. "He signs himself 'Badger' and addresses her as 'Kitten'."

Jack Tarrant grimaced with distaste.

"Yes, very frustrating. You know, Jack . . . ?"

"Hm?"

"One of the reasons I think you're such a wonderful lover . . ." he grinned, as indeed any man would have done in the circumstances – "is that you've never ever used any pet-name for me."

"Pet-names are for pets," he said gruffly.

Then he looked down at the handwritten page in front of him. "Good heavens!"

"What?"

"Listen to this." And, holding the old book up towards the flickering light of the mantelpiece candles, he read:

OF THE PUZZEL PECULIARITIE

That there be in the Puzzel Family in the Shire of Gloster a Peculiaritie in the Conformation of their Partes no longer admitteth of Doubt, for it is an Opinion that is not only vulgar, and common among the superstitious at present, but hath been delivered of old by ancient Writers, as witness diverse Chroniclers and authenticke Philosophers in the Countrie of France, where under the auncient Name of La Poucelle, the Family had its proper Origin, before its Arrival in this Lande in Companie of William Conqueror. But the Opinion that this Deformitie be a randomly maligne Influence, casting about it in every Direction the noxious Fumes of Evil, like unto the Stare of the fabled Gorgon or of the Cockatrice, is but a Fabrication of illiterate Heads; for there be no Record of Malignitie wrought by Members of the Puzzel Family upon others, but lamentable Testimony from many effectuall Authorities of much Discord and Destruction visited by Members of the Puzzel Family upon their consanguineous Relations. Whether this be meerely an atavisticke familial Humour, or a Coincidence of Misfortune generated by an inauspicious Configuration of the Zodiacke, or whether truely these sad

44

Histories can be traced by direct Line to the Puzzel Defor-mitie, is a Question beyond the Competence of the present Writer to be answerable. Doubt howsoever is there none of the veritable Existence and Continuation of a congenitall Deficiencie or Incompleatnesse in the Right Foot of all Puzzels, contrarie to the general Rules of Anatomie, as ob-served by Aristotle, Pliny and many pre-eminent Physitions. Let superstitious Mindes pass Judgement on the Puissance of this Odditie or Quirke of Nature, whether it be truely for Good or Evil, since the present Writer will side with neither, preferring better to be a meere Observer of the Phe-nomenone; and, as suche, will state incontrovertibly this Facte, affirmed by so many and varied Witnesses that it may not be a legitimate Objecte of Unbelief: *For many generationes all Members of the Puzzel Family have been borne with one Great Toe and but three Lesser Toes.*

"Well, he got to the point eventually," said Maria.

"Yes," Jack agreed thoughtfully. Then he looked at his watch. "We'd better be getting along for the Midnight Mass."

"You're expecting another clue there?"

"Wouldn't surprise me. No, I think we should make sure that at least one of us is present at every single event on the Christmas Break programme."

"Right."

"Apart from anything else, this is our first opportunity to have another look at the scene of the crime."

"Yes."

"Though I'll lay you any money you like, that Roddy Stout has been through the place, and everything in the chapel has been put neatly back to normal."

Jack Tarrant's surmise proved correct. The Puzzel Manor chapel gave no indication of having been the scene of a murder. The Puzzel shield was back in its ancestral position on the wall, and the whole space was tastefully garnished with holly and lit by candles. On the top row of the hymn indicator board, a "3" and an "0" had been set.

The service itself was something of a disappointment, at least for Bob and Barbara Hood. They had been told so much about the English traditional Festival of Nine Lessons and Carols – and indeed had heard the live radio broadcast from the Chapel of King's College Cambridge that afternoon – that they had assumed it to be the pattern for all Christmas services. To find that Midnight Mass was simply a Communion enlivened by four carols let down their expectations. They didn't see why the whole thing couldn't have been dressed up a bit. They had come all the way from California, after all.

The Rev. Verdure, however, was a traditionalist. Whether or not Roddy Stout had mooted to him the possibility of a more elaborate service Jack and Maria had no means of knowing, but what he delivered was a straight-down-the-middle Midnight Mass. The carols sung were "Once in Royal David's City", "Hark! the Herald Angels Sing!", "In the Bleak Midwinter" and "O, Come All Ye Faithful!" These were printed on special sheets, which were set out on the shelves of the pews when the congregation arrived.

There was a surprisingly good turn-out, given the national level of irreligion in England. Clearly the guests at Puzzel Manor did not represent a statistical cross-section of the country. Or perhaps it was just seasonal piety. Traditionally, more people turn out for church at Christmas than at any other time of the year, probably on the principle that they should perform some act of penance before giving themselves over wholly to self-indulgent consumerism.

The Stouts were present, and so was Nerys. The only guests not there were Lady Deathridge and her companion Trudy Bastable, who had opted for an early night. More significantly, in the light of the letter Maria had found, Celia Tranmere was also absent. If she was off pursuing her passionate liaison, then by a process of elimination Jack Tarrant deduced that "Badger" must be the one male in the house he had yet to meet – the chef, Anders Altmidson. But he had no proof that that was the case.

Colonel Honeycutt had allowed his son to stay up long past his normal bedtime for the Midnight Mass, presumably on the premise that a church service was character-building. Alexander's demeanour made it clear that he attended a traditional, God-fearing school. He knew when to stand, sit or kneel; he knew the responses; and he sang the carols confidently in a fine alto which would soon be ruined by his voice breaking.

The rest of the congregation was less familiar with the routine of church, and their small numbers made for a ragged unison both in responses and in singing.

Maria Lethbury was, needless to say, the shining exception to this general trend. Nobody had commented on her sudden recovery from the earlier migraine, and she was certainly justifying her presence in the chapel. She had spent much of her childhood in her father's cathedral choir, and she sang in a thrilling contralto which, on the rare occasions when he heard it, never failed to move her lover profoundly.

Her strong, firm speaking voice led the responses and, her father's daughter, she was instinctive on standing, sitting and kneeling. Which was why Jack Tarrant, incapable of any such movements, was surprised when, following one sequence of prayers, she stayed on her knees long after the rest of the congregation had risen to their feet.

The explanation came when he saw her transfer a piece of paper she had found beneath the pew in front to the capacious sleeve of her dress, and caught the slight wink of her eye. But they would have to wait till the end of the Midnight Mass before they could examine her find.

It was at this point in the service that Jack Tarrant was first struck by the oddity of the hymn board. The board itself was not out of place in a chapel; it was the "30" that had been slotted into its top row that didn't fit. Since all the carols were on the printed sheets, what was the point of giving a hymn number? And why was there only one?

Surreptitiously, he reached forward to a hymn book on the ledge in front. Maria gave him a look of reproof; in spite of her own recent example, she didn't approve of lapses of concentration in church.

But, undeterred, he opened the hymnal and riffled quietly through. Page 30 was a disappointment. He was about to put the book down when he noticed that the hymns themselves were numbered. He turned to number 30 and saw, in the top right-hand corner of the page, the symbol that he had both hoped for and feared. He slipped the book into his jacket pocket.

At the end of the service, the Rev. Verdure, in a procession of one, marched out of the chapel. Some of the congregation did a half-hearted kneel-and-pray routine before they too filed out. Jack wheeled himself up towards the altar, but the space beneath the Puzzel shield had been scrupulously tidied. There was no sign that, only six hours before, a murder victim had lain there.

In the candlelit passage outside the chapel, the Rev. Verdure stood, shaking the hands of his departing congregation, for all the world as if he were standing outside his own parish church in Puzzel Moultby. Roddy Stout was at his side, urging him to stay the night if he wished to – and indeed to stay for Christmas Day. The Puzzel Manor ovens, the proprietor assured him, worked on calor gas, so the power cut would not threaten the gastronomic delights of the morrow.

But no, the Rev. Verdure said, he'd try and get back to the vicarage. Liked to sleep in his own bed. And, he added, rubbing his hands with pioneering glee, he quite relished the challenge of crossing the snow again after dark.

Jack Tarrant, alive to every nuance of potential suspicion, found it very hard to imagine that the clergyman was anything other than what he seemed. That could be a wrong assumption, of course – given the levels of deviousness that he and Maria had already encountered at Puzzel Manor – but for the time being he was prepared to believe it. He was also a little comforted by the thought that, through whatever trials the next two days might offer, the Rev. Verdure would be only half a mile away. What a pity that the vicarage telephone wasn't working.

Back in the Yellow Room, Maria Lethbury drew the paper she had found from her sleeve.

"No – this first," said Jack, opening the hymn book. "This has got a bit of the coat of arms on it."

"How did you know where to find it?"

"On the hymn indicator. And at least it's the right hymn. 'Once in Royal David's City'."

Maria looked down at the music. She hadn't sung in a choir all that time for nothing. "Well, pretty obvious what's wrong there."

"Right," Jack agreed. "I've already worked it out. Three words."

And he wrote those three words down in the appropriate square of his shield diagram.

646

Once in royal David's city

Irby 878777

Words: C F Alexander (1818–1895)
Music: H J Gauntlett (1805–1876)
arranged A H Mann (1850–1929)
verse 6 arranged with descant Paul Edwards

SOPRANO
ALTO

1. Once in roy-al Da-vid's_ ci-ty Stood a low-ly cat-tle_ shed,
Where a mo-ther laid_her_ ba-by In a man-ger for_ his_ bed:

2. He came down to earth from hea-ven Who is God and Lord of_ all,
And his shel-ter was a_ sta-ble, And his cra-dle was a_ stall;

TENOR
BASS

Ma - ry_ was that mo-ther mild,- Je - sus_ Christ_ her lit - tle child._
With the_ poor and mean and low-ly Lived on_ earth_our Sa-viour ho - ly.

3. And through all his wondrous childhood
   He would honour and obey,
   Love and watch the lowly maiden,
   In whose gentle arms he lay:
   Christian children all must be
   Mild, obedient, good as he.

4. For he is our childhood's pattern,
   Day by day like us he grew,
   He was little, weak, and helpless,
   Tears and smiles like us he knew:
   And he feeleth for our sadness,
   And he shareth in our gladness.

5. And our eyes at last shall see him,
   Through his own redeeming love,
   For that child so dear and gentle
   Is our Lord in heaven above;
   And he leads his children on
   To the place where he is gone.

6. Not in that poor lowly stable,
   With the oxen standing by,
   We shall see him; but in heaven,
   Set at God's right hand on high;
   Where like stars his children crowned
   All in white shall wait around.

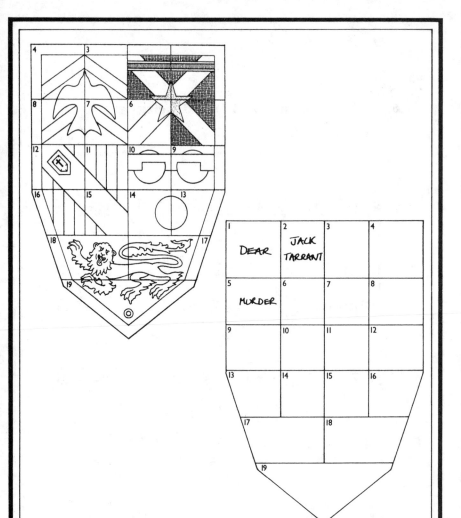

The grid on the right contains:

1 DEAR	2 JACK TARRANT	3	4
5 MURDER	6	7	8
9	10	11	12
13	14	15	16
17	18	
19	

THIS IS HOW MARIA LETHBURY HAD WORKED OUT THE THIRD PUZZLE:

Taking her cue from the title "The End of the Line", she had looked for the last letter of each line of text to find the solution.

FIVE

CHRISTMAS DAY –
12.30 A.M.
MINCE PIES

"He's teasing us," said Jack Tarrant. "Feeding it to us piecemeal. He's a bastard."

"Or she," said Maria. "Might be she."

He gave her a brief grin. "Is that a feminist response? Are you demanding equal representation for women as murder suspects?"

"No need. That's one area where women have always more than held their own – both in writing about murder and committing it."

"True. 'More deadly than the male', and all that. Anyway, you're right. Could be a man or a woman. Whoever it is, though, we're up against a mind that's devious and vicious and fundamentally evil."

"Let's look at what *I* found now." She held up the piece of paper that had come from the chapel. Then she sniffed at it. "Faint whiff of mothballs . . . Just like there was on the murder victim's suit. Could mean it came from his pocket."

"Could do."

Maria smoothed out the piece of paper on top of the fireside table and moved a candle from the mantelpiece so that they could see it more clearly.

The paper was crumpled and its fold lines were heavily marked, as if it had been kept in a pocket for a long time.

The words were typed on a piece of plain writing paper. There was no address or date.

Maria looked into Jack's grey eyes. "Well, let's assume for a minute that this did fall out of the dead man's pocket . . ."

"All right," he agreed cautiously.

"Now, on the whole, people tend to carry about letters that are addressed to themselves . . ."

"Not a universal rule, but let's go along with it for the time being."

"So we could therefore deduce that the murder victim's name begins with an 'A'."

"Possibly."

Her red hair shook with annoyance. "Oh, Jack, you're so pussy-footed!"

"Years of experience have taught me the importance of not leaping to conclusions. If I hadn't leapt to the conclusion that I could outwit 'The Executive Exterminator', I wouldn't be in this bloody chair now!"

"No. Sorry. Well, let's just for the moment assume that the dead man's name did begin with an 'A' – all right?"

"If you like. Doesn't help us a great deal, though. It's the only thing we *do* know about him."

"Well, this letter does offer at least two possible reasons why someone would have wanted to murder him. Whoever wrote the letter to him –"

"Possibly his brother – depending on how literally you want to take the 'fraternally'."

"All right, for the time being let's say 'his brother'. 'His brother' was also covertly threatening to expose something from the dead man's past to 'other people who will be at the manor house over Christmas'. That sounds like blackmail to me."

Jack Tarrant thoughtfully tapped a finger against his teeth. "Doesn't quite work, though, does it?"

"What do you mean? Murdering someone to stop them from

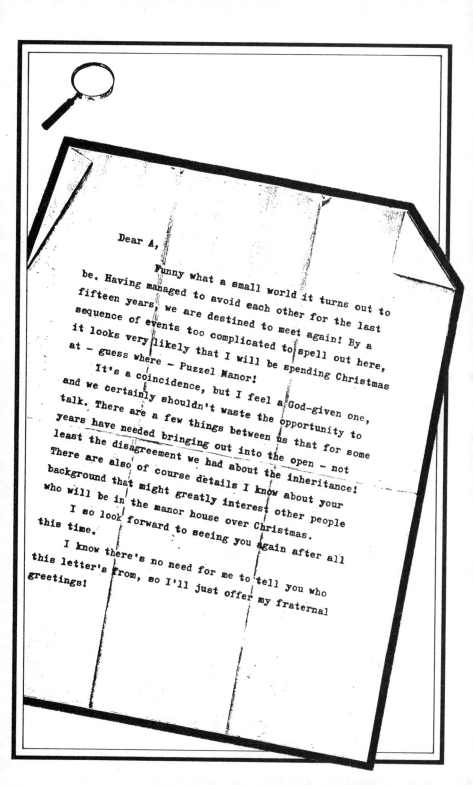

Dear A,

Funny what a small world it turns out to
be. Having managed to avoid each other for the last
fifteen years, we are destined to meet again! By a
sequence of events too complicated to spell out here,
it looks very likely that I will be spending Christmas
at - guess where - Puzzel Manor!

It's a coincidence, but I feel a God-given one,
and we certainly shouldn't waste the opportunity to
talk. There are a few things between us that for some
years have needed bringing out into the open - not
least the disagreement we had about the inheritance!
There are also of course details I know about your
background that might greatly interest other people
who will be in the manor house over Christmas.

I so look forward to seeing you again after all
this time.

I know there's no need for me to tell you who
this letter's from, so I'll just offer my fraternal
greetings!

blackmailing you is one of the oldest crimes in the world."

"Yes, but it would mean that 'A', our dead man, whatever we want to call him, would have had a motive to kill someone else – in other words, the person who was blackmailing him. From the blackmailer's point of view, it was to his advantage to see that 'A' stayed alive. The minute he was dead, there ceased to be any profit in blackmailing him."

Maria looked downcast. "You're right, of course."

"I think we need to know a bit more about our murder victim," Jack Tarrant announced. He looked at his watch. "What do you say to the idea of a little expedition in the wee small hours, Maria . . . ?"

"To the ice-house?"

He nodded. "We need to see if there's anything else in his pockets, see if we can find any clues in his clothing . . . and we also need to check exactly how he was killed."

"You don't think it was the Puzzel shield falling on him?"

"It could have been. I wonder, though . . . I am rather coming round to the theory that he might have been killed somewhere else and then moved to the chapel for dramatic effect."

"What gives you that idea?"

"I was just thinking about how cold his body was."

"It's very cold weather. A corpse is going to lose its body heat much quicker in conditions like this than under normal circumstances."

"Yes, but I was struck by the fact that the body felt colder than the ambient temperature in the chapel."

Maria caught on immediately to what he was saying. "You think he might have been kept in a freezer?"

"It's a possibility. Or in weather like this you could get the same effect by just storing the body anywhere outside the house."

"Yes. When do you want to go to the ice-house?" she asked eagerly.

"In two or three hours, when everyone's settled down for the night. First, though, I think we ought to go and try some of the Puzzel Manor mince pies."

*

56

The "Mince Pies and Nightcap" part of the programme was being held in the Hunters' Bar, off the entrance hall. As they went through, Jack and Maria saw Count Leo Leontchy sitting on his own in front of the fire where Trentham Metcalfe had read the Ghost Story. The foreigner, his monocle firmly screwed in, was working out a game of Patience on a low table. He looked up and smiled a polite greeting. If he was enjoying the benefits of cocaine, he did not allow it to affect his natural decorum.

In the Hunters' Bar, the guest list had trimmed down. Bob and Barbara Hood were being inducted into the mysteries of traditional mince-pie-eating, as Roddy Stout showed them how to lift off the top crust, put in a dollop of brandy butter, and replace the lid. As he did this, the proprietor patiently ran through the history of the delicacy: how originally the pies had been filled with minced meat; how, before the Civil War, they had been oblong, to represent the crib, sometimes even with a pastry baby on top of their crust; how Oliver Cromwell had banned them from English Christmas tables as symbols of idolatry; how eating one every day from Christmas to Twelfth Night was supposed to guarantee twelve happy months; and so on. All this he did to a cooing chorus of "Do you hear that, Bob?"s and "How about that, Barbara?"s.

Trentham Metcalfe, Celia Tranmere and Peggy Smith-Brously, meanwhile, were resolutely getting drunk. The two thespians exchanged theatrical anecdotage by the yard. Each time they mentioned a well-known name, Peggy Smith-Brously capped it with another, even-better-known name who had been "a great chum" of her late husband. Derek Smith-Brously, according to his widow, had been an amalgam of every available virtue. Tall, handsome, intelligent, he had distinguished himself hugely in "civic affairs", and only "departmental jealousies" had kept him from the knighthood he "so richly deserved".

As Jack and Maria arrived, the trio at the bar had just been supplied with another round of drinks by Jan Stout – Bailey's Irish Cream for Peggy Smith-Brously, Courvoisier for Celia Tranmere and, predictably enough, Scotch for Trentham Metcalfe.

Roddy Stout had looked up nervously as Jack wheeled himself

into the bar. He knew that either the detective or his girl-friend could ruin the Christmas Break whenever they chose, and seemed relieved that they didn't immediately make a public announcement about the body in the chapel.

Jan Stout asked the new arrivals what they would like to drink. Both ordered Laphroaig malt whisky.

After his first sip, Jack Tarrant commented casually that the Stouts were lucky all their guests had made it to Puzzel Manor, given the weather conditions.

"Yes," Jan agreed. "Done all right, haven't we?"

Maybe she'd been drinking, too. She was certainly sufficiently relaxed to let her syntax and her vowels go.

"So no absentees at all, are there?" Jack had already had this question answered by Roddy, but thought a pose of ignorance might elicit more information.

"Just the one." She dropped her voice rather elaborately and jerked a blonded head towards Celia Tranmere. "Friend of hers supposed to be coming. Presumably couldn't get through the snow. Actually," she murmured through closed teeth, "Madam seems rather upset about it. I mean, they was booked into separate rooms and that, but . . ." she winked – "say no more."

"Don't know what his name was, do you?"

"Oh, I'd have to look in the book. Unusual name. 'Anton' something, was it?"

"Ah."

Maria took up the baton of diffident interrogation. "Gather some of your staff couldn't get through the snow?"

"Right. Bit of a blow. What with that and the power cut and . . ." The proprietress recollected who she was talking to. "Not of course that the guests will suffer in any way. It'll still be the full Christmas Break, exactly as in the brochure."

"I'm sure it will be," said Maria comfortably. "So you're having to manage, just you and Roddy and Nerys . . . ?"

"Well, and Anders in the kitchen, of course."

"He makes a really good mince pie," said Jack, who was just sampling one.

"Oh yes, Anders is brilliant," Jan Stout enthused. "We were so lucky to get him. He's won lots of awards and had offers from the top restaurants in the country, but no, Puzzel Manor was where he wanted to work. Virtually volunteered his services to us, you know."

"Ah," said Jack lightly, as if the information wasn't very significant. "I look forward to meeting him."

And he really meant that.

"So it's just the four of you and the twelve guests, all cut off by the snow. Very cosy." Then Maria added, with only the slightest of interrogative inflections, "Nobody else at Puzzel Manor . . . ?"

"No," Jan Stout agreed.

Then *who* was the body in the chapel? The thought went through Jack and Maria's minds simultaneously, but neither voiced it.

"It must be very hard," said Jack sympathetically, "doing it all, manning the Reception and everything . . ."

"Oh, you're right there. And this weather's the last straw. This morning we were out there shovelling, trying to keep the main drive clear."

"All of you?"

"Well, not Anders. He'd got too much to do in the kitchen."

"Hm. And none of the guests arrived while you were all out there, did they?"

"No, I don't think – ooh, actually, now you come to mention it, a taxi did come and deliver someone while we was shovelling, because I remember Roddy saying he reckoned it was the last vehicle that was going to get up the drive till the thaw come. Mind you, he hadn't reckoned on Colonel Honeycutt's Range Rover."

"No. So . . . the taxi just deposited its passenger and went away again?"

"That's it."

"You don't know which of the guests it was who arrived then?"

"No, I don't . . ." She giggled. "But it must have been one of them, mustn't it? Names all in the book at Reception."

Jack nodded. "If the rest of you were all out there, who would have checked the newcomer in?"

"Well, Anders. The bell from Reception sounds in the kitchen

59

as well as the office, so he would have heard it. You can't have any problems of demarcation in a small business like this. No, Anders would have welcomed the new arrival, got him to sign in and then shown him to his room."

"Or her room," said Maria with a sweet smile.

But it was another alternative that suggested itself to Jack. That arrival in the taxi sounded like the only time the murder victim could have come to Puzzel Manor. Suppose Anders Altmidson had recognised him . . . ? Suppose he hadn't signed him in and shown him his room . . . ? Suppose he had shown him something else . . . ? A rather unexpected kind of welcome?

More than ever, Jack Tarrant wanted to meet the chef.

"Oh, have you really got to go? Have another drink," a slurred voice pleaded.

It was Celia Tranmere, whose drinking companions had all decided to call it a night. Bob and Barbara Hood were also going to "hit the hay". They all left in a flurry of Christmas wishes.

The actress looked desolated. She thrust her brandy balloon aggressively towards Jan Stout. "Well, I'm going to have another drink. You join me? *Anyone* join me?"

The Stouts apologised that they had things they must sort out, but Jack and Maria were delighted to accede to the offer. Jan poured a large Courvoisier and two large Laphroaigs before leaving with her husband.

"Be back in a little while to see if you want more drinks. Stay as long as you like. We'll be up for quite a time yet."

The intonation in her voice was skilfully judged. While in no way sarcastic, it still managed to imply that the Stouts didn't really want to be up manning the bar all night.

Celia Tranmere took a long swallow of her brandy. "Sodding men," she said, and started to cry.

This did not improve her already raddled features. Maria Lethbury was instantly feminine and solicitous, circling an arm round Celia's shoulders and producing a handkerchief to mop up the tears. "Do you want to talk about it?"

"It's just men . . . always the bloody same. You find one who things seem to work with, and then the bastard . . . doesn't turn up!"

This prompted another operatic wail and more cuddles and reassurance from Maria.

"What's his name, Celia?"

"Anton. Bloody Anton. He's not English, you know, he's foreign. And he was meant to be turning up here, and we were going to spend Christmas together and have nice cuddles and . . ." (she'd clearly been at the brandy most of the evening) ". . . and then he doesn't bloody turn up!"

"Maybe he couldn't get through the snow?" suggested Maria soothingly.

"Got as far as Puzzel bloody Moultby," Celia wailed, "because he rang me from there this morning – do I mean *this* morning? – yesterday morning . . . Christmas Eve morning. I was staying with a chum in Cheltenham, and Anton rang me there. About ten in the morning. Said he was in Puzzel Moultby and the road to Puzzel Manor was still passable and he was longing to see me and . . . And then my chum from Cheltenham drove me over just before lunch and we just made it through the drifts, and he went off and I looked round the hotel and found . . . the bastard wasn't here!"

This crescendo was followed by more there-thereing and tear-mopping from Maria. She caught Jack Tarrant's eye and read in it the "Let her run" message.

But Celia Tranmere had never needed a prompter in her professional life, and certainly didn't now.

"The bastard! Got cold feet, didn't he? When it came to it, he got cold feet. Whereas, in fact . . ." she started to become maudlin and nostalgic – "he had nice warm feet . . . funny feet, but nice warm feet." Her voice became babyish as she started to chant,

> "*This little piggy went to market,*
> *This little piggy stayed at home,*
> *This little piggy had roast beef,*
> *This little piggy had none.*
> *And this little piggy* . . . didn't do anything . . . because he
>   couldn't . . ."

Jack Tarrant raised an eyebrow to his girl-friend. At the same moment Celia Tranmere swayed and, but for Maria's prompt action in grabbing her arm, would have fallen off her chair. She had suddenly gone as limp as an empty glove puppet.

"I'd better get her up to bed."

Jack nodded. "See you in the Yellow Room."

Maria Lethbury expertly manoeuvred the drunken woman out of the Hunters' Bar. Jack Tarrant reflectively drained the last of his Laphroaig, and then wheeled himself slowly after them.

The main entrance hall was empty now. The fire had nearly died and the candles were guttering low. As Jack wheeled himself past, he noticed that Count Leontchy's Patience cards still lay set out on the fireside table.

He glanced at them, and almost moved on, but then stopped and looked more closely.

It was unlike any game of Patience he had ever seen before.

Apart from anything else, it seemed to have used three decks of cards.

And then, in the middle of the patterned back of the top card, Jack Tarrant saw the symbol that identified this as the next of the Puzzel Manor puzzles.

He took out paper and pencil, and began to work it out.

After a couple of minutes, he smiled dourly, and filled three words into the relevant space of his shield grid.

"The trouble is," he said half-aloud, as he lay wearily back in his wheelchair, "– you're bloody right!"

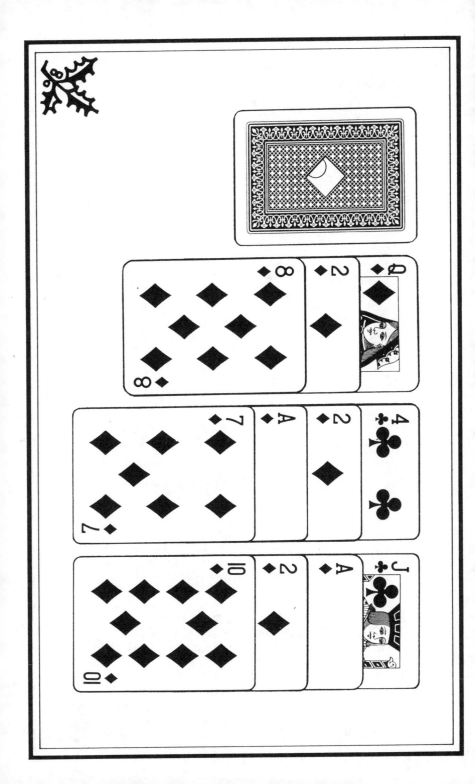

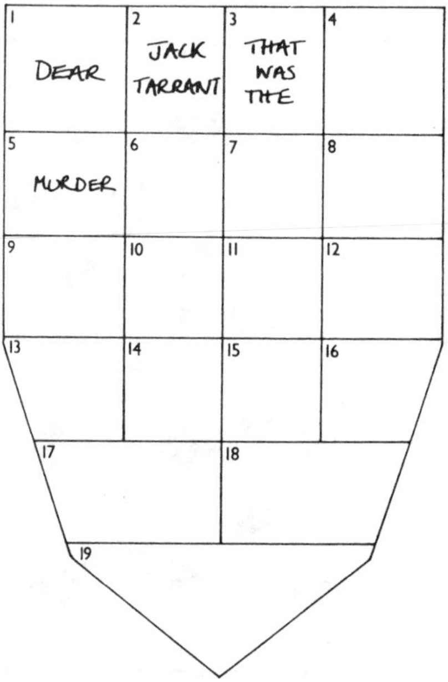
DEAR
JACK TARRANT
THAT WAS THE
MURDER

THIS IS HOW JACK AND MARIA HAD WORKED OUT THE FOURTH PUZZLE:

Knowing the tune of the carol well, they noticed three errors in the music, where crotchets (blacked-in notes) had been replaced by minims (hollow notes). They looked for the words adjacent to these deliberate mistakes, and placed those words in order according to the number of minims (one for "that", two for "was", and three for "the").

SIX

CHRISTMAS DAY – 3.30 A.M. NIGHTCAP

J ack Tarrant wheeled himself down a long dark corridor. It was in a part of Puzzel Manor he had not visited before. The flames from spreading stubs of candles, ensconced at intervals along the walls, swayed like drugged dancers and threw their evanescent patterns against the low ceiling.

The chill he felt was not precisely fear, more an appalling certainty that he was about to be confronted by something terrible.

His eyes strained in the gloom and his ears in the silence, alert for any clue, any sliver of foreknowledge that might cushion a little the shock that lay ahead.

The corridor curved away and suddenly he saw that its end was sealed by a studded oak door, on which the words "Ice-House" had been hammered out in tarnished nails.

The parallel bolts, as thick as prison bars, had been drawn back. The ornate handle of a huge key protruded from the massive lock-plate at right angles to the slot, as if it had just been turned by some unseen hand.

Above this hung a broad iron ring. Jack reached out and

grasped it firmly. The metal was cold to his hand, almost cold enough to weld itself on to his skin.

He had expected the door to open outwards, but at his first touch it swung away out of his grasp, the scream of its hinges ripping through the silence. A blast of icy air hit his face with the force of a punch.

In his left hand he held a candle, which wavered madly on the verge of extinction in the sudden draught. But its flame righted itself and flared back. Tentatively, turning the wheel of his chair with his right hand, Jack Tarrant held the candle out into the frozen space.

The ice-house was higher than he had expected. Frozen spears hung down like stalagtites, converting the ceiling to a pagan cathedral, the trophy-hoard of some Gothic warlord, draped with the frigid banners of the vanquished dead.

And at the far end, where, had it been a cathedral, the altar would have stood, hung one human trophy.

A cold metallic taste rose in Jack Tarrant's throat as he wheeled towards the body. He felt shock and nausea, but no surprise. He had known for so long what he would find there.

The corpse was suspended from an ice-clad beam, facing the wall. It was stiff as a wooden doll, perhaps from rigor mortis or maybe just the cold.

The weight of the body had almost straightened out the kinks of black plastic-covered wire around its neck, but closer examination he knew would reveal the ligature to be the lead from a carphone.

Just as it had been with the others.

Just as it had been with the others, all the victim's hair had been shaved off, so close to the skin that it was impossible to tell what colour it had been.

And, just as it had been with the others, a neat slip of paper had been stapled to the back collar of the smart business suit.

"WITH COMPLIMENTS," it read, but this time the murderer had chosen to add, in typed letters, the soubriquet so tastelessly donated by the tabloid press, "FROM THE EXECUTIVE EXTERMINATOR."

Jack Tarrant was now directly beneath the corpse. He reached

66

up to a shoeless foot. The stockinged flesh felt ominously familiar, and panic rose in him.

He gave a little pull and felt the body's weight shift as it swung round to face him.

Hardly daring to do so, he looked up and saw, staring down at him, every fear of his entire life made flesh.

Made dead flesh.

Even through the crude slash of red lipstick and the smudges of bright blue eye-shadow with which the murderer had disfigured the previous victims, he could recognise the outline of the jaw.

And, even without the crowning glory of her hair, he knew he was looking into the face of Maria Lethbury.

Then he heard the laugh. The laugh he could never forget.

A scream rose within him, swelling, taking him over, blotting out everything else in his life.

And, as he screamed, his name was called out, hands gripped his shoulders and the brutalised face was forced down towards his. Closer, closer, closer –

"Jack! Jack! JACK!"

His eyes opened and the scream died on his lips.

Maria's face was close to his, but it bore no trace of the obscene make-up. And the beauty of her red hair cascaded down over him as she shook him awake.

"Jack! Jack, it's all right."

"Oh, Maria . . . Maria, you're here. You're all right?" His arms enfolded and crushed her to him, as though she were the only floating thing in an endless, ferocious sea.

"Of course I'm all right. Of course I'm here. Jack, I'll never leave you."

"No, I won't let you." He found he was sobbing. "And I won't let anyone take you away from me."

"Just let 'em try," she said, with a derisive laugh. Then, more softly, "Was it the same dream?"

He nodded. No need to tell her the appalling new variation, the new choice of victim. "Yes, the same dream."

"It'll pass. It will. Already they're getting much further apart.

It's nearly a month since the last one, isn't it?"

He nodded. "Trouble is, each time I think it's gone for ever and then, when it does come back, it's even more terrifying."

"It will go away for good, Jack."

"Yes. One day." He looked round the Yellow Room. The fire had burnt low. One candle on the mantelpiece gave out a pale light. "I didn't intend to go to sleep. I just lay down on the bed to be out of that bloody wheelchair for a few minutes and next thing I knew . . ."

"All that Laphroaig."

"Yes, probably. What is the time, anyway?"

"Half-past three."

"Half-past three on Christmas morning at Puzzel Manor. Hm." Jack Tarrant pulled the wheelchair towards him and eased himself off the bed into it. "Perfect time for a post mortem examination, I'd say."

Maria grinned and picked up her torch. "Perfect."

And as they left the Yellow Room, she murmured:

"'Twas the night before Christmas, when all through the
    house
Not a creature was stirring, not even a . . .' – corpse."

The reality of the ice-house was unlike the baroque fantasy of Jack Tarrant's dream.

Following the small spoor of Maria's pencil torch, the two of them had passed through the entrance hall and dining room into the Puzzel Manor kitchens. These were spotlessly modern, with much stainless steel in evidence, both on the surfaces and in the variety of utensils which hung in synchronised rows above the gas-fired range. Delicious spicy smells seeped out from under the larder door as the detectives passed through, promising that whatever other disasters Christmas Day might hold, the food at least would be wonderful.

Of the kitchen's master – or perhaps maestro – the brilliant Anders Altmidson, there was no sign. Even more Jack Tarrant wanted now to meet this mysterious figure. Was it just professional self-effacement that had kept the chef apart from the

68

guests? Or was there some other, more sinister, reason why he had not been seen?

The back door of the kitchen was locked, but the key had been left in the keyhole. As they opened the door, the sudden chill snatched at Jack and Maria's breath. The kitchen gave out on to a small covered yard, in which various supplies, barrels, crates and boxes, were neatly stacked.

Maria ran the beam of her torch across the wall opposite, which closer examination revealed to be cladding for an excavation into the hillside. The manor had been built into a fold of the Cotswolds, with the space behind dug out to give light to the back of the building.

Into the wall were set a pair of thick wooden doors with large fleur-de-lys hinges.

"Must be it," Jack breathed in Maria's ear. "Sort of place they would have put an ice-house."

"I've never really understood," she breathed back. "What was an ice-house for?"

"At the risk of sounding obvious, it was for ice."

"Thanks *very* much."

"No, seriously. Before the days of refrigeration, the only way you could get ice in the summer was to have kept it from the winter, when of course it was manufactured naturally. So you had to find – or more usually build – a place that was extremely well insulated to stop the stuff melting. That's why ice-houses tend to be underground or dug into hillsides like this one. Let's go and have a look."

Maria manoeuvred the wheelchair down the step into the yard, and Jack propelled himself smoothly across to the doors. Above them, the wooden covering to the yard creaked, protesting against its unaccustomed burden of snow.

The little circle of light from the torch found a padlock holding the doors shut. "One you can do?" asked Maria.

Jack chuckled. "Pretty standard, yes."

He reached into his pocket for the set of picks he always carried with him, instinctively selected the right one, and sprang the lock as easily as if he'd been using a key.

He pulled at one of the doors and Maria the other, laying them gently back against the wall. She sprayed torchlight down into the void. "A few steps, I'm afraid."

"You'd better take me down them."

It was a routine they had done many times before. He tipped himself back in the wheelchair as Maria pulled on the handles. Balancing the chair at forty-five degrees and controlling its descent, she let the wheels bump down from step to step till they reached the stone floor, where Jack righted himself. Maria used extra caution for fear of losing her footing on the icy steps.

She ran her torch around the small, dank room. Its original purpose rendered redundant by electricity, the ice-house was evidently now just used as extra storage space. Conference chairs were neatly stacked along one side. Three croquet sets, four garden umbrellas and six folded loungers were propped against the other, waiting for summer. And at the far end were cots, for guests who arrived with small children.

They were all of the same design, with solid panels at head and foot, and barred sides, one of which could be raised and lowered to facilitate picking up the child within. Most had been dismantled, their components stacked in neat piles, but one cot was assembled.

And in that, his limbs spilling out incongruously like a man in a wheelbarrow, lay the murder victim.

The cot's panels were decorated with a frieze of bunny rabbits and teddy bears, designed no doubt to soothe its juvenile incumbent into sleep. But not into quite such a permanent sleep as the current occupant was enjoying.

He looked perhaps paler than he had in the chapel, but otherwise exactly the same.

Wordlessly, Jack took the torch from Maria and moved its beam slowly along the contours of the corpse.

The nearside arm hung nonchalantly over the rail, as if its owner were trailing his hand in water from the side of a boat. But not much of the hand could be seen. It was almost eclipsed by the sleeve of his jacket.

Jack Tarrant went closer and pulled the material taut. The hand disappeared completely.

"No way this is his own suit."

"Mm?"

"Look, the sleeves are far too long for him." Jack wheeled smartly down to the end of the cot and pulled at a ruckled-up trouser leg. At full stretch, it almost covered the black-shoed foot. "These trousers are so big, he'd have tripped over if he tried walking in them."

As usual, Maria was keeping up with his thought-processes. "You mean the suit was put on him after he was dead?"

Jack nodded. "I'd say almost definitely."

He leant closer, and sniffed the fabric of the trouser leg. "Smell of mothballs still quite distinct. I think it's a long time since anyone living wore this suit."

"Could you just shine the torch on his head?"

Jack obliged, and Maria, without a vestige of squeamishness, moved close to the victim's crushed skull. "Yes, as we suspected, this dog-collar and bib is absolutely brand-new."

"Anything useful on the suit itself? Labels, that kind of thing?"

Maria fumbled inside the dead man's jacket. "You hoping for a little tag reading, 'Tailored exclusively for Mr A. Murderer, 17 Murderer's Row, Peckham Rye, London SE15'?"

"Something like that, yes. Any luck?"

"Marks and Spencers," Maria read flatly.

"Oh. Oh well, nice idea."

"I'll read you the washing instructions, if you like," she offered.

"Sweet of you, love, but don't bother."

"Shall I check through his pockets again? Might have missed something."

"May as well."

Jack sat thoughtfully in his wheelchair while Maria did a thorough check, but her searches produced nothing. "No," she concluded, "I think that notebook was all we were meant to find."

"And the letter under the pew."

"Yes. I wonder if that had actually dropped out of his pocket or not."

"Doesn't really matter. Either way we were definitely meant to find it."

"Yes . . ." Maria shivered. "It's horrible, isn't it, the thought

71

that someone is orchestrating this whole thing for us, feeding out little gobbets of information. It makes me feel so powerless. We can't do anything for ourselves, can't initiate anything. We just have to play the game at his pace."

"Or *her* pace."

"Sorry. That should be my line, shouldn't it?"

Jack sat at the end of the cot, lost in thought. The dead man's legs, which in life would have hinged at the knees, stuck up into the air, unnaturally stiff above the transfers of bunny rabbits and teddy bears.

"Bring the torch round here. I've had a thought." Maria came to join him. "Now shine it on his shoes. First the right one . . . then the left. And again. First the right . . . then the left." A light of triumph glowed in Jack Tarrant's eye. "Notice anything odd?"

"Well, the two shoes appear to be different sizes."

"Exactly. Or at least different widths. The right one is definitely narrower than the left."

"Yes."

"So what do you reckon that means?"

"Could mean that whoever dressed the body in the suit and dog-collar couldn't find a matching pair of shoes that fitted him . . . ?"

"Could mean that. I don't think it does, though. If you look at the shoes, they appear to be a very good fit. An exceptionally good fit, as if they had been made for this particular pair of feet. A pair of feet of different sizes."

Maria shrugged. "Lots of people's feet are different sizes. There was a girl I used to sing with in the cathedral choir who . . ."

"Never mind that," Jack interrupted excitedly. "Take his right shoe off."

Maria did as she was told and handed the shoe to Jack.

"Now the sock."

She stripped the sock off too.

"Now shine the torch on his foot."

"Good heavens!" Maria Lethbury murmured.

"Yes, good heavens!" Jack Tarrant agreed. "Now we are getting somewhere, wouldn't you say?"

The foot illuminated in the torchbeam was just the kind of foot one would expect to find on a dead man in his fifties.

Except for one detail.

It had only four toes.

"'The Puzzel Peculiaritie'!" Maria murmured.

"Yes . . ."

"Do you think this means he is actually – *was* actually a member of the Puzzel family?"

"I'd put money on it. It makes sense of a whole lot of things."

"Including his identity, Jack."

"Hm?" For once he was slower on the uptake than she was.

"Do you remember what Celia Tranmere said when she was talking about her lover?"

"What she chanted, you mean?"

"Yes, Jack. Exactly. '*And this little piggy* . . . didn't do anything . . . because he couldn't . . .'."

"How does the original rhyme go?"

"'*This little piggy ran wee-wee-wee all the way home.*'"

"Yes. I knew it was something pretty inspirational. It's a rhyme mothers use when they're counting their babies' toes, isn't it?"

"Yes."

"I must say, the idea of grown men and women using it as a form of foreplay is pretty repellent."

"Jack, the kind of couple who call each other 'Badger' and 'Kitten' are capable of levels of tweeness we cannot begin to imagine."

"True. So . . ." He looked across at the cot. "*Requiescat in pace*, Anton."

"Do you think his surname was 'Puzzel'?"

"Well, if it was, I'm sure he called himself something else for Celia's benefit . . . and indeed for booking in at Puzzel Manor. Someone would have been sure to mention the coincidence otherwise – wouldn't they?"

"Yes."

Jack suddenly became businesslike. "Right, we don't want anyone to realise we've been in here, so we'd better put poor Anton's shoe back on and . . ."

He stopped, transfixed by something he saw inside the shoe on his lap. He reached in his hand and pulled out a folded sheet of paper.

Maria peered over his shoulder as he opened it out.

"Oh no!"

"Oh yes, Maria. Oh yes. Look, there's the bit of the coat of arms. This is the next puzzle all right."

She shuddered. "That means the murderer knew we were going to come down here. It's horrible. It's as if he's reading our minds."

"Or *she*'s reading our minds."

Jack Tarrant looked down at the verse in front of him. "Hm, looks a bit tricky ... I don't quite see the way into this one."

Maria Lethbury also studied the typewritten lines. There was a long silence. Then she said, "Oh yes. I think I see . . ."

"Well, I don't." Jack sounded rather grumpy. Then a new thought cheered him. "Annabelle! Didn't we hear Trudy Bastable call Lady Deathridge 'Annabelle'? And Lady Deathridge is a 'noblewoman', isn't she? Is that what it means?"

"It *might* do," said Maria cautiously, "though it's not the line I'm working on."

"You are so helpful sometimes. Can't you give me a clue?"

"You have to take it literally," Maria explained.

"Literally?"

"Yes. It's also significant that you've got 'o – apostrophe' rather than 'of' in the third line."

"Is it really?"

"And the answer," she added helpfully, "is a five-letter word."

"Thanks, but I don't see how you get to that five-letter word."

"Well, like most puzzles," said Maria Lethbury, "you solve it by a process of elimination."

"Thanks," said Jack Tarrant, sounding grumpy again. "Thanks a bundle. That really *does* help."

Maria smiled. "Do you want me to tell you what the answer is . . . ?"

"No! No, certainly not!"

NOblewoman

Bane of men, O Annabelle ~
Abominable name!
All men beware o'Annabelle ~
Annabelle's to blame!

THIS IS HOW JACK WORKED OUT THE FIFTH PUZZLE:

Having noticed that the Patience game only used two suits, Clubs and Diamonds, and remembering that each suit contains thirteen cards, Jack realised that this allowed a potential total of twenty-six cards. This number is significant because it is also the total number of letters in the alphabet. Taking the suits in alphabetical order, he then, starting with the Ace of Clubs to represent "A", the Two of Clubs "B" and so on, found values for the cards left on the table and was able to fill in his answer.

SEVEN

CHRISTMAS DAY – 8.00 A.M. STOCKING OPENING

"Happy Christmas, darling."

Jack Tarrant's eyes opened and looked up into Maria Lethbury's. He felt the warmth of her body and the opulence of her hair brushing his cheek, and he prayed that he would be lucky enough always to wake up to the same sight.

This, however, was hardly proper waking-up. Neither of them had done more than doze fitfully since their excursion to the ice-house. Jack, in his sleeping moments, had not been troubled by the recurrent nightmare, but the thoughts which came to him each time he woke were hardly more appealing.

It was the knowledge that the murderer was playing with him that hurt. And what he had secretly feared had now been spelled out. The threat had been implicit in the answer to the last puzzle. Unless the murderer could be stopped, there would be more violent deaths at Puzzel Manor before the Christmas Break was over.

Jack Tarrant grinned ruefully up at Maria. "Happy Christmas, darling."

"I know what you're thinking," she said. "I've been thinking the same."

"I just feel so powerless," said Jack bitterly. "He – or she – is running circles round me, and here I am stuck in that bloody wheelchair!"

"That has nothing to do with it, Jack. This isn't a physical contest, it's a mental one. It's your mind that's being challenged, not your body. And I have great confidence in that mind of yours. Doing all those endless crosswords in hospital wasn't wasted – it means now you're at the peak of training. He or she may think he or she's very clever, but he or she's up against someone even cleverer."

"I'm touched by your loyalty to me, Maria, but –"

"I didn't mean *just* you, you pompous ass. I meant the two of us together. That's a world-beating combination. Don't worry, we'll get the better of him."

"Or her."

"Or her."

Maria collapsed gently on top of her lover, and he held her in a long hug. Then they drew apart. Nothing had been said, but there was a tacit agreement between them that they would not make love again until the case had been solved.

He reached under the pillow and produced a small silver-wrapped package. "Happy Christmas," he said, as he handed it to her.

Maria took it with one hand and slipped the other under her pillow to produce a golden envelope. "Happy Christmas, Jack."

The bracelet was unwrapped and on her wrist and he was being smothered with kisses of gratitude before he had time to open his envelope. When her ecstasy subsided, he drew out the card inside and studied it.

"Some people, Maria," he said with a grin, "would regard that as a sick joke."

On the card were details of the membership she had arranged for him at an exclusive golf club.

"Well, then 'some people' would be very stupid," said Maria with spirit. "I *know* you're going to get better. The surgeon said two more operations."

"He said two more operations and I might be able to *walk*. I don't recall him saying too much about my playing golf."

78

"You will. I have complete faith."

And her complete faith gave him, if not as complete a faith, at least a degree of hope. And reinforced determination. If Jack Tarrant stayed in a wheelchair for the rest of his life, then "The Executive Exterminator" would have won. And Jack Tarrant was determined that "The Executive Exterminator" would not win.

Maria pushed back the covers and leapt lithely from the bed. She tugged at the cord of the yellow striped curtains and the whiteness of the light seemed to sear away the silk of her nightdress, outlining the perfect contours of her body. Jack felt a surge of love for her. He could never leave her. He could never allow anything to happen to her.

"It's actually stopped snowing. Pretty deep, and the sky looks full of more, but at least for the moment it's stopped."

She waved to someone, and Jack, from the bed, craned upwards to look through the window. He was just in time to see the answering wave from Alexander Honeycutt. The boy was muffled in anorak, scarf and moonboots, and seemed to have shed about five years now he was playing in the snow.

He was building a snowman, and had already piled up a tapering white body almost as tall as he was. But the way he stumbled about in the snow and the depth to which he sank showed how treacherous the conditions still were.

Jack could see the yew tree by the main gates of Puzzel Manor, probably only five hundred yards away. But it would be a long and arduous five hundred yards to traverse, even for someone in peak condition. It was a journey that a man in a wheelchair could not even contemplate.

No, they were well and truly cut off. And with the phone lines down, there was no possible chance of summoning outside help. If there was any way of stopping the escalating violence at Puzzel Manor, Jack and Maria would have to find it for themselves.

"I had a thought . . ." said Maria, as she snuggled back into bed.

"Uhuh?"

"You know the body in the chapel – the body in the ice-house, if you prefer . . ."

"Mm?"

"And the letter we found, which smelled of mothballs as if it had come out of the suit he was wearing. . . well, you remember when we discussed blackmail, you said it didn't work, because there was no incentive to murder the blackmail *victim*, only the blackmailer himself . . ."

"Or herself."

"Yes. Now, if our dead body was wearing someone else's suit, then it's possible that whoever murdered him had put him into one of his own suits . . ."

Jack Tarrant's eyes gleamed with excitement. "And so the letter was actually *from* the murder victim rather than *to* him – is that what you were thinking?"

"It's exactly what I was thinking."

"Good girl. Yes, that's excellent." He pieced it together. "So, depending on our interpretation of that word 'fraternally' in the letter, it's possible that we're looking for Anton's brother – a tall man with a guilty secret. A secret so guilty that he was prepared to kill to keep it quiet."

"That's the way it looks . . ." Maria was thoughtful for a moment. "Colonel Honeycutt's pretty tall . . ."

"So, according to his widow, was the late Derek Smith-Brously. The lovely Peggy might have brought one of his suits with her . . ."

"Yes, and of course she's got the set of kitchen knives. If the next victim is killed with a kitchen knife –"

"Maria, we're going to try and ensure that there isn't a 'next victim'."

"Yes, I know, but I wonder if –"

Maria was interrupted by a knock on the door. Their shout of "Come in" admitted a very apologetic Nerys, who was carrying two bulging Christmas stockings.

"I'm so sorry. You were meant to have had these earlier."

"Oh. Aren't you a bit . . . improperly dressed, Nerys?"

The long black hair swayed as she looked down at her dark blue business suit in some confusion. "I don't think so, Mr Tarrant. All my buttons are done up and –"

"No, I was meaning – shouldn't you be wearing a red coat and white beard?"

A beam spread over her face. "Oh, right. Yes. No, what happened was . . . originally Mr Stout was going to dress up in the gear and go round in the middle of the night putting the stockings on people's beds, but then he decided some of the guests might be a little upset to have strange hooded figures creeping round their rooms in the dark . . ."

Given the propensities of one of the figures who was already creeping round Puzzel Manor, the guests would have every reason to be upset.

"So the idea was that I should do the rounds early, give a quick knock on each door, and put the stockings on the beds . . . you know, before people woke up properly. Only I got a bit behind. Everything's really chaotic this morning."

"Any particular reason?" asked Maria casually.

"No, not really. It's just, you know, when you haven't got any power, everything takes that much longer. We're having to heat up water for the guests in the kitchen and Anders has got lots of stuff already on the stove and then there's breakfast to do and, well, you know . . . All basically fine, though," she concluded with professional optimism.

"Good."

"Breakfast in the dining room from eight thirty onwards. But no hurry. Turn up when you like."

"Thanks very much."

"Hot water will, as I say, be coming round soon. Erm, anything else you need?"

"Oh, one thing," said Jack. "Not for now, but later in the morning . . . I just wondered if there was any other information around about the history of Puzzel Manor and the Puzzel family? I saw that book that Trentham Metcalfe read from last night, but I wondered if there was anything else?"

"I think there are some files of stuff in the office behind Reception. You're welcome to come and have a look there, if you want to, Mr Tarrant."

"Thank you very much, Nerys. I probably will, after breakfast."

"Right." She moved to the door and then hesitated. "I'm sure there was something else I was meant to say . . ."

For a moment her face clouded. Then she remembered. With a broad smile, she said, "Yes, of course. Happy Christmas."

"Happy Christmas, Nerys."

The atmosphere at breakfast was quite jolly. After the traumas of arrival and the natural awkwardness (natural to the British, anyway) of being in unfamiliar company, the guests had settled down to enjoy themselves. Now it was clear that the Puzzel Manor management would not be fazed by the lack of electricity and telephone contact with the outside world, the paying customers could look forward confidently to the advertised pleasures of their Christmas Break.

And the spectre of murder had no power to chill the breakfasting guests because, by Jack Tarrant's reckoning, a maximum of three people in the dining room knew of that spectre's existence.

Maria and he knew of it, obviously . . . and so did the murderer.

Whether the murderer was actually in the room was a moot point. All the guests were there, except for Celia Tranmere. (She was presumably sleeping off the excesses of the night before – and, given the news of her lover's tragic fate, which she must find out at some point, it was perhaps as well she should sleep as long as possible.)

Nerys was acting as waitress, once again taking on with professional aplomb a task considerably beneath her executive qualifications.

The other potential murderers, Jan and Roddy Stout and the mysterious chef – perhaps the most intriguing suspect of all – did not put in an appearance during breakfast. The proprietors were making arrangements for the rest of the day's programme, while Anders Altmidson provided evidence of his existence in the form of mouth-watering croissants, fluffy scrambled egg, fragrant bacon, crisp fried bread and voluptuous black pudding.

The guests had appreciated their Christmas stockings, although conversation soon made it clear that all the men had received the same selection of goodies, as had all the women. Still, they agreed – in the phrase which has, from time immemorial, compensated for Christmas disappointments – "It's the thought that counts." And no one was so churlish as to observe that, at Puzzel Manor, they were paying very handsomely for that thought.

After breakfast, as she had promised, Nerys conducted Jack and Maria to the office and produced what there was of Puzzel family history – the leatherbound book that Jack had already inspected, and a couple of dusty and faded buff files.

"Do you mind if I leave you to it? Table's got to be laid up for lunch."

"No, that's great, thank you. You're doing a terrific job. Not all of it, I imagine, quite at the level you were trained for . . . ?"

Nerys gave him a wry grin. "One thing you learn very early in the hotel trade is that you have to be ready to turn your hand to anything. I'll see you later."

They watched her go, small, dark, efficient. "Is she on our list of suspects?" asked Maria.

"I'm afraid everyone is, until we identify the murderer."

"Hm. I'll be surprised if it's her. I like her. She's good, efficient, unflappable. I think she could go a long way in hotel management. I can't really see her being mixed up in a murder."

"No." Suddenly, an image crossed Jack's mind of a way Nerys could be mixed up in a murder. She looked the perfect executive in her neat navy suit; her hair was long and beautiful. The thought chilled him, and he did not confide it to Maria.

He looked round the office which, situated at the front of the house, was well lit by natural light. Heat was provided by a small open fire (there were advantages during a power cut of being in a building designed before the invention of central heating), but of course the lack of electricity rendered useless the gleaming new computer and fax machine.

He picked up the telephone and listened.

"Just checking," he replied to Maria's unspoken question. "If the line really is down, it might have been mended by now."

"And if it's not, the murderer might have conveniently forgotten to disconnect it again after his – or her – last call to his gang of homicidal henchmen . . . ?"

"Something like that, yes. But . . ." he replaced the receiver – "dead as a doornail."

He opened the leatherbound book and looked for the "End of the Line" puzzle. It had disappeared. The whole page had been neatly excised by a sharp blade. With a sigh, he passed the book across to Maria. "I looked through this last night, but you double-check. See if there's anything important I missed. I'll have a go at these files."

The buff folders were filled with all those scraps of paper that houseowners don't think they'll ever need, but equally don't think they should throw away. Old household bills, estimates for building work, odd sheets of accounts, letters from banks – a mixture of documentary oddments, some of whose dates went back over a century. It was material which would have proved of great interest to a social historian, or even a collector of ephemera, but not to the investigator of a murder.

Except for two items.

Amidst all the other, irrelevant ones, there were two bits of paper that didn't fit in. The first was part of a letter, the second a torn sheet of computer paper.

The letter appeared to have been written by some kind of genealogist or historian, and was clearly addressed to whoever owned Puzzel Manor in 1903. The writing was precise and academic, as was the style of the content. Only one page had survived from what had evidently been a much longer letter.

That was all that had survived, but it was enough to set Jack Tarrant's mind racing.

Grimly, he handed the document across to Maria, and turned his attention to the torn sheet of computer paper.

whether you would find it possible to
confirm, either from local oral sources or from
documentary evidence found within Puzzel
Manor, the rumour that the Puzzel family did
not die out with the death of Sir Henry Puzzel
in 1879.

The alternative version of events, taken from
the deathbed confession of an elderly woman who
had worked as a housemaid at Puzzel Manor,
suggested that the supposed self-inflicted deaths
by drowning of both Sonia Puzzel and her son
Gervaise were in fact elaborate deceptions,
instigated by the mother. The old lady maintained
that, instead of dying by their own hands at
Christmas 1877 and Christmas 1878 respectively,
the mother and son in reality staged their own deaths
and fled to the Continent, where they lived lives
of irredeemable wickedness. This, the dying crone
asserted, was the explanation for the fact that
neither body was found when the lake in the
grounds of Puzzel Manor was dragged, and
also for Gervaise Puzzel's supposed suicide note
which read, "I have gone to join my mother."

I have found other evidence which
might support this apparently outrageous
suggestion. I therefore implore you to make a
thorough examination of any papers relating
to the Puzzel family which may have
survived at Puzzel Manor in order

"Well, there seems little doubt about it," said Maria flatly when she had read the letter. "The rumour must have been true. The Puzzels *did* survive, and Anton must have been one of the current generation. He had the hereditary foot deformity."

"Yes. I wonder who else belongs to the current generation of Puzzels . . . ?"

"What's that other piece of paper?"

"Well, this –"

But he was interrupted by the reappearance of Nerys, who had come to tell them about an extra feature for the afternoon, "Presents round the Christmas Tree".

"Nerys, perhaps you can help me? I found this sheet of computer paper . . ."

She glanced across at it. "Oh, there are probably a good few around like that. The printer went completely bananas a few weeks back – was spewing up all kinds of garbage. I had to get the maintenance man in to sort it out. He explained what the problem was – needless to say, didn't mean a light to me – but the machine's been going fine since then, so that's all I care about. Anyway, must dash."

As Nerys left, Maria moved across to look over Jack's shoulder. "Certainly looks like garbage."

"Yes, and I would assume it was . . . except for the hand-written message. And that."

His finger pointed to the section of coat of arms at the bottom of the sheet.

"Being generous to us now, Jack – giving us two segments at once."

"Hm. I think we'll find that's as far as his or her generosity goes."

"Anyway, let's see if we can work out the puzzle."

"Yes," said Jack thoughtfully. "Will we be equal to it . . . ?"

ARE YOU EQUAL TO THIS ONE ?

Dear Paula,
I'm sorry I can't tell you exactly who will be
meeting your group that's arriving in Cheltenham for
the Christmas Break at Puzzel Manor next month.
Everything's still a bit chaotic here and I'm afraid
rather behind schedule. I seem to have been
victimised by bad weather, some unexpected dry rot,
non-appearing plumbers and generally uncooperative
British workmennnnnn@@@@$$$$$ ---££[[[[[[[?
[[[[[[[[[[
[[[%%%%%%%//////////asssttrirrrlllllHGDS=###   #### ##
jjjj&&&&&]]]**CVCVCCVCV\\DDWELL£££ £££££££££££klutz=
###!!!!///xxxMNMNMNM}}{{{{{OR>>>>>:Yyrew=####6675bfds
HKJSDFG,,,,<<¦¦<<<VVVVV^^^^^^^^^^^^^^^^xzXZ+++98555
HilgoPPPPPzzlllllllllllll****drippppminnnstr:::%%%%gbG=
#####??
???
????????????????????@@@@$$$$$ ---££[[[[[[[?

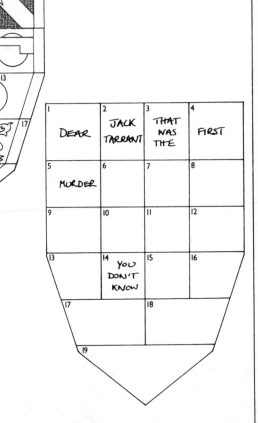

THIS IS HOW MARIA
WORKED OUT THE SIXTH PUZZLE:

She saw that the clue lay in the way the title was printed - "NOblewoman". Taking that literally, she read it as "NO", negating what followed. As she said, it was "a process of elimination". So there was NO "b", NO "l", NO "e", and so on. Once she had eliminated all those letters - b, l, e, w, o, m, a and n, she was left with the answer. (Jack got there too, but it took him a bit longer!)

EIGHT

CHRISTMAS DAY – 1.30 P.M. TRADITIONAL CHRISTMAS LUNCH

He was there, when the guests, animated by pre-prandial champagne, filed through into the dining room.

Anders Altmidson. The Danish chef. The one hitherto unseen piece in the puzzle of Puzzel Manor.

He was dressed in traditional chef's costume – tall white hat, white coat, spotted scarf knotted at the neck, blue checked trousers. And on his feet – perhaps a concession to his Scandinavian upbringing – heavy wooden clogs with black leather uppers.

He stood, with carving knife and fork at the ready, behind a glistening golden-brown bird, whose proportions seemed to qualify it better to be a roc or phoenix or some other mythical beast than a mere turkey. Around it on the table were steaming dishes of roast potatoes, mashed potatoes, pommes dauphinoises, Brussels sprouts, French beans, cauliflower cheese, petits pois, four different kinds of stuffing, rich brown gravy, bread sauce, cranberry sauce and a profusion of other sauces whose aromatic piquancies mingled to fill the room.

So splendid was the tableau that the entering guests broke into spontaneous applause, which the creator of all this magnificence acknowledged with smiles and nods of gratification.

Anders Altmidson appeared to be a man of great and unassuming charm, but Jack Tarrant and Maria Lethbury found themselves unable to respond to this. All they were aware of was the fact that he was exceptionally tall, that his hair was almost white, and that, on entering the dining room, Celia Tranmere (restored by the transfusion of champagne to something of her former vivacity) had stopped at the sight of him, as if he reminded her of someone. And indeed, for Jack and Maria too, there seemed to be a distinct resemblance between the handsome face of the tall chef and the crushed face of the body they had last seen in the ice-house cot.

Both of them felt a desperate urge to remove the clog from the man's right foot and confirm their quick-breeding conjectures. But clearly Christmas lunch was not the moment to do that.

The small tables, dispersed around the room for the previous evening's supper and that morning's breakfast, had now been amalgamated into one long central table. This was profusely decorated with holly, sprigs of fir, pine cones and silver ribbons, from whose undergrowth gleaming brass candlesticks rose. The parchment-coloured candles were all lit, and their mellow glow softened the snow-reflected daylight which blazed through the dining room's tall windows.

The place settings, each one fronted by a promising parade of wine glasses, winked in the candlelight. At the centre of each was a card bearing a guest's name in graceful sepia calligraphy, and at the side an opulently frilled cracker in red and silver or green and silver.

"What have we got here?" asked Bob Hood, picking one up as he sat down.

"It's a cracker," Lady Deathridge informed him.

"Cracker? What, you eat this? You mean inside the wrapping there's a cracker . . . a – what do you call it – a biscuit?"

"No, this is called a cracker. You pull it –"

"You *pull* it?"

"Yes, Mr Hood, you and the person next to you each take hold of one end and you pull it."

"And then what happens?"

"There's a bang, and you find that inside is a novelty of some kind, and a paper hat – oh, and quite often a joke or motto."

"Well, what do you know?" Shaking his head in amazement, he waved across the table to his wife. "Hey, Barbara, you know what this favour thing's called? It's a cracker."

"A *cracker*?" Barbara Hood echoed in disbelief.

But further discussion of this strange phenomenon was interrupted by the arrival at the table of Jan Stout with the first platefuls of perfect white turkey slices, which she distributed before returning to Anders' table for more. She was followed by Nerys with a tray of vegetable dishes and then her husband, bearing the alternatives of Sancerre and a rather good claret. Conversation became spasmodic, as the guests settled down to enjoy their traditional Christmas fare.

As he ate, Jack Tarrant looked covertly round the table. The level of cunning already shown by the Puzzel Manor killer meant that he and Maria were up against a virtuoso of deception. For such a character, maintaining the smokescreen of another identity would be, almost literally, second nature. So any one of these apparently ordinary personalities might be the mask for a murderer.

The Stouts' seating plan seemed to be working well and, in the intervals between actual mastication, few appeared to be at a loss for conversation.

The guest who had hitherto been the least communicative, Trudy Bastable, sat on Jack's left, and even she, removed from the inhibiting presence of her employer, Lady Deathridge, showed some signs of animation. She expressed an interest in Jack Tarrant's former career, and asked politely if his work had ever brought him to the Cotswolds. Did he have contacts in the local constabulary, by any chance?

Next to Trudy sat Count Leo Leontchy, neat, precise, courteous as always. He was seated next to Celia Tranmere, on whom the twinkle of his monocle and the powerful beam of his charm were firmly focused.

The actress, as ever, responded positively to masculine

attention. She became fluffy and coquettish. "Oh, yes," Jack overheard her saying on a ripple of giggles, "when it snows, my whole personality changes."

On Celia's other side sat Alexander Honeycutt, totally unworried by the fact that she was ignoring him. This was partly because he was engrossed in his food as only a thirteen-year-old growing boy can be (he'd insisted on having one of the turkey's legs, which almost eclipsed his plate), and partly because his other neighbour, Barbara Hood, kept asking him for new details of British Christmas lore, which he was happy to supply. It was a refreshing change for him to be treated as an informed adult.

Beyond Barbara Hood sat Trentham Metcalfe, rubicund with wine. In fact the redness of his face and the whiteness of his hair made Jack certain that the two days would not be allowed to pass without the actor putting in an appearance in the red gown and white beard of Santa Claus. It would be perfect type-casting.

Trentham was shamelessly chatting up Nerys, who sat beside him, reacting with good humour to his ponderous gallantries, which were constantly interrupted as she had to leap up and minister to the needs of the guests.

All the Puzzel Manor staff sat that end of the table, the Stouts determined to maintain the illusion of a family Christmas, even though their guests had paid a considerable amount to be part of that particular family. Roddy and Jan, seated beyond Nerys, like her had to keep getting up to serve someone with more food or wine. They did not have much opportunity to eat or drink themselves.

Nor did the chef. Anders Altmidson was seated next to Jan Stout, but constantly returning to the turkey, from which, with a surgeon's precision, he removed more perfect slices for the hungry guests.

In his rare moments of respite, he seemed to be chatting amiably enough to Lady Deathridge, who listened with a condescending patrician smile.

For her, the only people in the world of real interest were those of her own class. People who aspired to her class, but hadn't the proper breeding to back up their pretensions – people, in fact, like Peggy Smith-Brously – she despised. All the rest of the British population she dismissed as simply "common" and, as for foreigners . . . well, they were "foreign", which said it all. The idea that she had spent Christmas lunch exchanging badinage with *a Danish chef* was an amusing incongruity which would be much brought up amongst her bridge friends over the ensuing months.

And when she told those friends that on her other side had been an American . . . well, what hilarity that would provoke! Americans, in Lady Deathridge's view, were even more common than "other ranks" British, but their inability to grasp this truth was almost endearing. So she listened politely to Bob Hood's assertions of all the things he liked about England, salting away some of his quainter inanities to be produced to loud upper-class laughter at a later date.

Maria sat between Bob, whose ingenuous enthusiasm she much enjoyed, and Colonel Honeycutt, whom she did not find such an easy companion. He seemed a very tense character, who took the traditional reserve of the military man to a ridiculous degree. When Maria casually asked whether Alexander lived with his mother, all she got by way of reply was, "Mother dead. Boy at boarding school most of the time. With an aunt during holidays."

Nicely brought up by the bishop and the actress, Maria Lethbury persevered with a few more conversational overtures, but since they all got similar shorthand answers, she at last gave up and directed her attention exclusively to Bob Hood.

Peggy Smith-Brously, on the Colonel's other side, found conversation with him equally tough going, and so spent most of the lunch talking to Jack Tarrant. Since her conversation consisted largely of repeating what a very important man her late husband Derek had been, and what a poisonous woman Lady Deathridge was, and how difficult it was to buy shoes if your feet were anything other than a standard size, Jack had little difficulty in switching off and maintaining the illusion of attention by a few reflex "Ah"s and "Really?"s.

So his thoughts were free to concentrate on the murder and the identity of its perpetrator. He felt convinced the killer was sitting at the same table with him and, though all his suspicions

93

seemed to point in one direction, Jack Tarrant was too wily an old bird to rule out any possibility at this stage of an investigation.

The turkey course was finally finished and expertly cleared away. Then the curtains were drawn and the candles snuffed (though this was hardly necessary since renewed snowfalls had brought daylight to a premature end), and everyone was silenced for the entrance of the Christmas Pudding.

Jack and Maria were particularly alert in the darkness. They now knew another murder was planned; they were also beginning to understand the murderer's sense of the dramatic.

And when Anders Altmidson entered, bearing in front of him a salver, for a horrible moment the flaming object it contained looked to Jack Tarrant like a human head.

But no, he was over-reacting, letting the paranoid atmosphere get to him. The object on the salver was just a pudding – traditionally made, cooked wrapped in a cloth, and now presented in a traditional blue halo of burning brandy.

Nerys followed the chef with a dish of mince pies, and bowls of cream and brandy butter. The candles were rekindled, and the guests embarked on their sweet course.

Maria was also tense, fearing some new horror in the pudding itself. But all the rich, dark mixture contained was the traditional bonus of cash. The Stouts had invested in old silver threepenny bits for the occasion, and Maria was delighted to find that her slice contained three.

Everyone was by now bloated and mellow – in the case of the two thespians, on the drunken side of mellow – and a pleasing lethargy had crept over the party.

Stilton and Bath Oliver biscuits were produced, but only Alexander Honeycutt had the capacity left to do them justice.

Then came nuts and fruit. Then coffee. Port and brandy were circulated and imbibed.

There was no doubt that, in spite of the weather, the power cut, and the dark shadow of murder (of which shadow most of the guests could be presumed to be unaware), the main meal, the focus of the Puzzel Manor Christmas Break, had been an unqualified success.

It was Bob Hood, through the comfortable apathy of over-indulgence, who remembered the crackers.

"Hey, come on. We got to see what's inside these babies. Isn't that right, Barbara?"

"Certainly is, Bob. We never seen one of these in the States. Now, what's the procedure with them?"

"Well, the ideal way to pull crackers," said Roddy Stout, ever ready with more Christmas tradition, "is for everyone to cross arms, holding a cracker in one hand, take the other end of their neighbour's cracker, and all pull together."

"Sounds like the 'Eton Boating Song'," commented the slurred voice of Trentham Metcalfe.

British reserve had by now melted to the extent that no one refused to participate and, after a few false starts, a good deal of giggling, and some prudent moving of wineglasses, all sixteen at the table had their arms crossed and had formed a human chain of crackers.

"It's a bit like the way you sing that song on New Year's Eve," Alexander Honeycutt enthused. "You know, 'Old Lamb Stew'."

"'Auld Lang Syne'," said Barbara Hood gently.

"Oh. Yes."

"Right, are we all ready?" demanded Roddy Stout. "On a count of three then. One – two – three!"

Thirty-two arms tugged in unison. A fusillade of snappers sounded. Amidst giggling, shrieking and scrambling on the floor, the guests retrieved their party hats, found and swapped their novelties, read and groaned at each other's jokes.

Only Jack Tarrant was still and stern-faced.

He did not look at the paper hat his cracker had contained. Nor at the miniature screwdriver set. He just looked at the motto.

It was more of a riddle than a motto. And a small design in the top right-hand corner identified it as something more sinister than just an ordinary riddle.

He studied it fiercely for a moment, then looked around covertly to see if anyone was watching his reactions.

But no, the murderer was too canny for that. Everyone seemed caught up in the general mood of hilarity.

Jack Tarrant returned his attention to the riddle. "Well, the answer's two words . . ." he thought. "And there's definitely a red herring. Now, given what I know about the way my adversary's mind works, is he – or she – likely to repeat himself – or, come to that, herself . . . ?"

WHAT AM I?

My first is in first, but not in second
(Unless in Roman numerals reckoned).
Really my second's a blank, a lacuna,
Dead ground, or nothing – an M if you'd sooner.
Easy my third – it's in fate, but not fortune,
Read but not red, impart not importune.

When you've got these, my fourth will be next
(Even thirteenth in a certain context)
At least in America it's bound to show.
Perhaps the Mid-West . . . ? In a western, no.
Only my whole now – above from the end –
Not quite your target – confuse a French friend.

1 DEAR	2 JACK TARRANT	3 THAT WAS THE	4 FIRST
5 MURDER	6	7	8
9	10 WHO WILL BE THE NEXT VICTIM?	11	12
13	14 YOU DON'T KNOW	15	16
	17	18	
		19	

THIS IS HOW JACK AND MARIA WORKED OUT THE SEVENTH PUZZLE:

They noticed that the layouts of the coherent part of the letter and of the gibberish part matched exactly. Taking the clue the murderer had given them in the word "equal" ("Are you <u>equal</u> to this one?"), they looked for the equal signs in the computer gibberish, and noted that each was followed by a sequence of # signs. Matching these up with the identically positioned words in the coherent text, they found their solution.

NINE

CHRISTMAS DAY – 6.00 P.M. DICKENS BY THE FIRESIDE

"It is of course very difficult," said Count Leo Leontchy in his cautiously exact English, "for someone who was brought up as I was to come round to the idea of women being in charge of anything important."

"Well then, it's about time you were dragged into the twentieth century," Maria Lethbury retorted.

"I know, I know. I must do it, but it is not natural for me. My late wife, the Countess, would have had a heart seizure if one even mentioned the idea of her having to *do* anything. But then, of course, I grew up in a different culture. I mean, I am aware that great advances have been made in this country. For many years you even had a woman Prime Minister . . ."

"Yes, I don't think she was actually much of an argument. She didn't advance the cause of *other* women at all, just of herself. But . . ." Maria's cheeks flushed as she warmed to her theme – "it should be clear now, at the latter end of the twentieth century, that there is absolutely no job that cannot be done at least as well by a woman as by a man."

"Assuming, of course," Lady Deathridge murmured icily, "that a woman has to work in the first place."

"Well, what on earth's she going to do with her life if she doesn't *work*?" Maria demanded.

Lady Deathridge was sourly silent.

A slight sourness had crept over everything since the end of the meal. It was just reaction after the drink and self-indulgence. Maybe it would have been better if the Stouts had scheduled a rest period for the afternoon. To hope that the lunchtime bonhomie would continue straight into the jollity of "Presents round the Christmas Tree" had perhaps been over-optimistic.

Not that the presents themselves had not been appreciated. It was the manner of their dispensation that maybe left something to be desired. This had been undertaken by Trentham Metcalfe, dressed finally, as nature had always intended him to be, as Santa Claus.

Unfortunately, it soon became apparent that his festive heartiness derived from spirits other than the seasonal kind. He just about managed to read the names on the tags and give all the guests the correct gifts, before subsiding into an armchair, whence his stentorian snores now reverberated through the entrance hall.

The archetypal Christmas scene – a group of people gathered round a blazing fire, candles winking from a tall spangled fir-tree – was rather let down by the presence of a hopelessly drunk Santa Claus.

Still, in a very British way, no one passed comment, and the desultory discussion of feminism continued.

"I think," said Peggy Smith-Brously, who had come to regard it as a point of honour to disagree with Lady Deathridge at every opportunity, "that there is nothing worse than the idea of a 'lady of leisure'."

"Yes, well, that is exactly what I would have expected someone of your background to think," Lady Deathridge observed superciliously.

"It's horses for courses," said Jan Stout, trying to dilute the developing atmosphere. "Some women enjoy work, some need to work, and some don't feel the necessity."

"You, I assume, Mrs Brously-Smith, have always needed to

work." Lady Deathridge's intonation was more poisonous than ever.

Peggy Smith-Brously was deeply affronted, not least by the corruption of her name. Only a person whose surname actually includes a "Smith" and a hyphen can be properly sensitive to the immense social gulf between those who have the hyphen before the "Smith" and those who have it after.

"Of course I didn't *need* to. My late husband Derek made so much money that I need never have lifted a finger throughout my married life. But I thought I had something to *contribute*. It was charity work, of course. I wouldn't have dreamt of accepting any payment. One doesn't even think of the money."

"Well, there are some women who have to think of the money."

Trudy Bastable's uncharacteristic assertiveness was immediately shrivelled by the Medusa stare of her employer.

Celia Tranmere decided that she had been silent too long. "For me, the problem's been *finding* the work. I've always been ready, but the way the theatre's going these days, there's nothing about."

"Does what actresses do count as *work*?" asked Lady Deathridge, determined, it seemed, to antagonise as many people as possible.

Then she received support for her side of the argument from an unexpected source. Colonel Honeycutt suddenly announced in his customary shorthand, "Lot of trouble caused by women working. Late wife, Vanessa, Alexander's mother, tried to keep a career going. Didn't do her any good. Still be alive if she'd stayed at home, like women should."

"But, Daddy, it wasn't Mummy's fault. It was just unbelievably bad luck that she happened to be –"

"Quiet, Alexander!"

The boy was obediently silent, but the exchange had set a new train of thought racing through Jack Tarrant's mind. The third victim of "The Executive Exterminator" had been a woman called Vanessa Dickinson. Jack himself hadn't been involved in the post-murder interviews with her husband, but he remembered that the man had been in the army. Was it possible that

101

Alexander Honeycutt's mother had been Vanessa Dickinson?

Damn. He wished he had access to "The Executive Exterminator" files. He wished he had access to a telephone to check with someone who did have access to those files. But he didn't.

Maybe the Christian name was just a coincidence. Maybe he was leaping to conclusions.

But the thought, once released in his mind, was a deeply disquieting one. And it raised a follow-up question: Did any of the other Christmas guests at Puzzel Manor have connections with "The Executive Exterminator"'s victims?

"Well, I think," said Barbara Hood comfortably, "that there's room for work, and there's room for leisure, for men and for women. Bob and I both worked hard till we retired, and now we have more time to travel and generally enjoy life. I mean, here we are drinking in all the delights of a traditional English Christmas, and last summer we were also in Europe, touring Scandinavia, tracing Bob's family history, and I guess we couldn't have afforded that kind of stuff if I hadn't worked . . . so I reckon, you know, you find what's right for you."

"Like I said – horses for courses," Jan Stout agreed.

"I think it's more than that," said Nerys with sudden pugnacity. "I think women should work, push themselves to the limit, get as far as they can in their careers. Men have made the rules for too long."

The suddenness of this outburst surprised them all. Maybe it was the lunchtime drink which had made the Assistant Manager drop her professional mask. There was no doubt, though, that what she said was heartfelt.

And her views received enthusiastic support from Maria Lethbury. "Exactly. That is it. Women have got a lot of ground to make up. There is absolutely no reason why a woman should not be at least as effective a manager as a man in any area of business you care to mention."

"So long as she remains like a woman."

The new voice was foreign, soft and slightly sing-song. No one had noticed the chef, Anders Altmidson, his long body stretched over a settle outside the fireside circle.

"What do you mean?" asked Maria.

"I mean that by all means, for sure, women should have good jobs, do well – this is all fine, of course. But they should also keep their femininity."

"You mean they should dress well and – ?"

"This is good, of course, and important, but it is not everything. Women who are in jobs should keep the gentle nature which is the mark of a woman."

"Not sure that gentle nature *is* the mark of a woman," Colonel Honeycutt grunted. "Not always my experience."

"What exactly do you mean, Anders?"

"What I mean, Miss Maria Lethbury, is this – that women should behave, for sure, like women even in men's world. They should not become bad-mannered and aggressive."

"No, of course not, but –"

Now the chef was under way, he was not going to be stopped until he had had his say. "I work till little while ago in London restaurant. There we have many women customers – women who, for sure, are successful – they must be, of course, to afford the prices. Many of them behave very badly. They call chef out of the kitchen and complain very rudely. Many smoke over my food!"

Though the voice retained its sing-song delivery, the passion within it was growing. "These women have stopped being women. They are not good! They want to be in a man's world, for sure . . . All right, of course. But if they behave so aggressive, they must not be surprised to be the victims of aggression!"

He seemed to stop very suddenly, and there was an awkward silence. Nothing the chef had said before had prepared anyone for such depth of emotion. By the end, his speech had become a tirade. He had sounded out of control, almost unhinged.

Jack looked across at Maria, and could see that their thoughts coincided.

"Well . . ." said Jan Stout, realising that something soothing was required of her in her hostess role and falling back on the universal British panacea. "Anders, I'm sure some of our guests would like a cup of tea. And how about some of those lovely little biscuits you made . . . ?"

"Yes. Yes, of course," the chef grunted, uncoiling his long

body from the settle. He set off towards the kitchen.

"Anyway," the proprietress continued, "what we're meant to be doing now is listening to some Dickens, isn't it? Trentham was going to read to us about Mr Pickwick's Christmas at Ding-a-Ling."

"Um, I think it's Dingley Dell, actually," said Alexander Honeycutt with schoolboy precision.

"Yes, yes, course it is. That's what I meant. Trentham . . . Trentham. Trentham!"

The actor was nudged out of sleep and looked blearily about him. "Is it my cue?" he asked, totally fuddled.

"You were going to read us some Dickens," said Jan Stout coldly.

"Ah, Dickens, yes." Trentham Metcalfe chuckled heartily. "Did you ever hear that joke: 'Do you like Dickens?' – 'I don't know, I've never been to one!'"

"I'm afraid I don't understand that," said Lady Deathridge.

"Well, 'Dickens' – sounds like 'Dick-Ins' . . . you know, back in the sixties you used to have 'love-ins' and 'sleep-ins' and – "

"I think if you could just *read*, Trentham." Jan Stout's voice dropped a few more degrees as she handed across the copy of *Pickwick Papers*.

"Oh yes, right. Now where – ?"

"There *is* a marker by the relevant chapter."

"Yes. Oh. Right." He peered at the page, as if it was written in a foreign language, and then launched in:

"'CHAPTER TWENTY-EIGHT: A good-humoured Christmas Chapter, containing an account of a wedding, and some other sports beside; which, although in their way even as good customs as marriage itself, are not quite so religiously kept up in these deg . . . degen . . . degenerate times . . .'"

The trouble he had with "degenerate" was nothing to the problems that "Pickwickians" in the first sentence caused him, and he had great difficulty getting his tongue round the rest of Dickens' seasonal schmaltz.

"'Christmas was close at hand,'" he slurred, the words sliding out of control like smooth-soled shoes on ice, "'in all its bluff and hearty honesty; it was the season of hospitality, merriment, and open-heartedness; the old year was preparing, like an ancient philosopher, to call his friends around him, and amidst the sounds of feasting and revelry to pass gently and calmly away. Gay and merry –'"

The appearance of Anders Altmidson, announcing that there was tea in the Hunters' Bar for anyone who might want it, was a welcome relief. The guests instantly started to melt away, none wishing to prolong the embarrassment of the reading. Some went for tea, some said they were going to have a little lie-down, while Jan Stout led Trentham Metcalfe off, beginning his hissed dressing-down even before they were out of the room.

Jack Tarrant and Maria Lethbury lingered by the fire. Both had observations and new ideas they wanted to discuss. As he waited for the room to clear of other guests, Jack idly turned the pages of the copy of *Pickwick Papers* from which Trentham Metcalfe had so inexpertly read.

He stopped and stared at a page. "Oh no."

Maria looked down at the book. "Oh *yes*. Giving us three segments this time – more generous than ever."

"Yes," said Jack, as they concentrated on the page in front of them. "Well, I don't think this should delay us too long . . ."

Long before Mr. Pickwick was weary of dancing, the newly-married couple had retired from the scene. There was a glorious supper down-stairs, notwithstanding, and a good long sitting after it: and when Mr. Pickwick awoke, late the next morning, he had a confused recollection of having, severally and confidentially, invited somewhere about five-and-forty people to dine with him at the George and Vulture, the very first time they came to London; which Mr. Pickwick rightly considered a pretty certain indication of his having taken something besides exercise on the previous night.

"And so your family has games in the kitchen to-night, my dear, has they?" inquired Sam of Emma.

"Yes, Mr. Weller," replied Emma; "we always have on Christmas-eve. Master wouldn't neglect to keep it up on any account."

"Your master's a wery pretty notion of keepin' anythin' up, my dear," said Mr. Weller; "I never see such a sensible sort of man as he is, or such a reg'lar gen'l'm'n."

"Oh, that he is!" said the fat boy, joining in the conversation; "don't he breed nice pork!" and the fat youth gave a semi-cannibalic leer at Mr. Weller, as he thought of the roast legs and gravy.

"Oh, you've woke up at last, have you?" said Sam.

The fat boy nodded.

"I'll tell you what it is, young boa constructer," said Mr. Weller, impressively; "if you don't sleep a little less, and exercise a little more, wen you comes to be a man you'll lay yourself open to the same sort of personal inconwenience as was inflicted on the old gen'l'm'n as wore the pigtail."

"What did they do to him?" inquired the fat boy, in a faltering voice.

"I'm a-goin' to tell you," replied Mr. Weller; "he was one o' the largest patterns as was ever turned out—reg'lar fat man, as hadn't caught a glimpse of his own shoes for five-and-forty year."

"Lor!" exclaimed Emma.

"No, that he hadn't, my dear," said Mr. Weller, "and if you'd put an exact model of his own legs on the dinin' table afore him, he wouldn't ha' known 'em. Well, he always walks to his office with a wery handsome gold watch-chain hanging out about a foot and a quarter, and a gold watch in his fob pocket as was worth — I'm afraid to say how much, but as much as a watch can be—a large, heavy, round mana-facter, as stout for a watch as he was for a man, and with a big face in proportion. 'You'd better not carry that 'ere watch,' says the old gen'l'm'n's

friends, 'you'll be robbed on it,' says they. 'Shall I?' says he. 'Yes, will you,' says they. 'Vell,' says he, 'I should like to see the thief as could get this here watch out, for I'm blest if *I* ever can, it's such a tight fit,' says he; 'and venever I wants to know what's o'clock, I'm obliged to stare into the bakers' shops,' he says. Well, then he laughs as hearty as if he was a-goin' to pieces, and out he walks agin with his powdered head and pigtail, and rolls down the Strand vith the chain hangin' out furder than ever, and the great round watch almost bustin' through his grey kersey smalls. There warn't a pickpocket in all London as didn't take a pull at that chain, but the chain 'ud never break, and the watch 'ud never come out, so they soon got tired o' dragging such a heavy old gen'l'm'n along the pavement, and he'd go home and laugh till the pigtail wibrated like the penderlum of a Dutch clock. At last, one day the old gen'l'm'n was a rollin' along, and he sees a pickpocket as he knows by sight, a-comin' up, arm-in-arm vith a little boy vith a wery large head. 'Here's a game,' says the old gen'l'm'n to himself, 'they're a-goin' to have another try, but it won't do!' So he begins a chucklin' wery hearty, wen, all of a sudden, the little boy leaves hold of the pickpocket's arm, and rushes headforemost straight into the old gen'l'm'n's stomach, and for a moment doubles him right up vith the pain. 'Murder!' says the old gen'l'm'n. 'All right, sir,' says the pickpocket, a-wisperin' in his ear. And wen he comes straight agin, the watch and chain was gone, and what's worse than that, the old gen'l'm'n's digestion was all wrong ever arter-vards, to the wery last day of his life; so just you look about you, young feller, and take care you don't get too fat."

As Mr. Weller concluded this moral tale, with which the fat boy appeared much affected, they all three repaired to the large kitchen, in which the family were by this time assembled, according to annual custom on Christmas-eve, observed by old Wardle's forefathers from time immemorial.

From the centre of the ceiling of this kitchen, old Wardle had just suspended, with his own hands, a huge branch of mistletoe, and this same branch of mistletoe instantaneously gave rise to a scene of general and most delightful struggling and confusion; in the midst of which, Mr. Pickwick, with a gallantry that would have done honour to a descendant of Lady Tollimglower herself, took the old lady by the hand, led her beneath the mystic branch, and saluted her in all courtesy and decorum. The old lady submitted to this piece of practical politeness with all

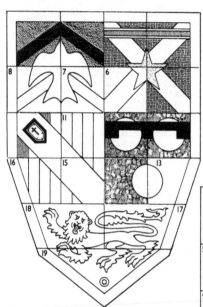

1 DEAR	2 JACK TARRANT	3 THAT WAS THE	4 FIRST
5 MURDER	6	7	8
9 WHO WILL BE THE NEXT VICTIM?	10	11	12 I AM
13	14 YOU DON'T KNOW	15	16
17		18	
19			

THIS IS HOW JACK SOLVED THE EIGHTH PUZZLE:

He quickly rejected the red herring, "MURDER WEAPON", which was written in capitals down the left hand side of the verse, on the grounds that the murderer had already used that device in "The End of the Line" puzzle. That meant it was the riddle itself that needed solving.

The first letter had to be "I" - contained in the word "first" and in "second" when written in Roman numerals ("II").

The second was, as the verse said, a "blank", indicating a space between words (or an "M", which is a unit of space in printing).

The third was clearly "A" - contained in the words "fate", "impart" and "Read", but not in "fortune", "red" or "importune".

The fourth was "M", the thirteenth letter of the alphabet, contained in the word "Mid-West", though not in "western".

And the last couplet gave three distinct clues to the whole phrase: "above from the end" signified that the answer was in the last two words of the title, "WHAT AM I?", taken from the back; "Not quite your target" indicated that the answer was an anagram of "AIM"; and "confuse a French friend" indicated an anagram of "AMI". Phew!

TEN

CHRISTMAS DAY – 8.30 P.M. PARTY GAMES

"God, I hate the way he's playing with us!" Jack Tarrant snapped. "He's teasing us, treating us like idiots, calmly telling us his plans – as if we can do nothing about it!"

"And do you think there's a lot we can do about it?" asked Maria calmly.

"Not at the moment, no. We haven't got enough to go on. And he knows that. He's playing on that fact."

"I notice the 'or she' seems to have dropped out of your calculations."

"Yes. Well, it's . . . I don't know. Everything seems to be pointing in the same direction."

Her red hair glistened in the candlelight as Maria nodded. "It does seem pretty obvious, doesn't it?"

"Yes. Maybe too obvious . . ."

"Well, shouldn't we just go and tell Roddy Stout . . . give up trying to do the whole thing on our own . . . share the problem, before there's any further bloodshed?"

Jack grimaced and shook his head. "If we do that . . . well, for one thing, I reckon Roddy Stout'd do anything to shut us up on the subject. He doesn't want his precious Christmas Break disrupted – even by murder – so he's quite capable of locking us up to keep us quiet. There is also another danger . . ."

"Namely?"

"Well, we've agreed how obvious the identity of the murderer seems to be at the moment . . ."

"Yes?"

"Given the way we're being manipulated, it's quite possible that what we're thinking is *so* obvious that it's exactly what the murderer wants us to think."

"You mean misdirecting our suspicions is just another of his vicious games?"

"It'd be in character. I wouldn't rule out the possibility. I wouldn't yet rule out anything. Or anyone."

"Even Roddy Stout, you mean?"

Jack nodded and absent-mindedly riffled through the copy of *Pickwick Papers* that still lay on his lap.

Maria shuddered. "It's horrible, isn't it – knowing that another murder has been promised, knowing that there's another innocent victim at Puzzel Manor whose life is about to be cut short?"

"Don't be so pessimistic. It'll only be cut short if we don't manage to stop the murder. And I certainly haven't written off that possibility yet."

"No, of course not." But a shadow of defeatism lay across Maria Lethbury's usually positive face.

"Good God, what's this?"

Tucked in the pages of the old book, Jack Tarrant had found a newspaper cutting.

"Has it got part of the coat of arms on it?"

"No, but still doesn't mean we weren't meant to find it. I'm pretty sure this was planted here for us, just like everything else."

The scrap of newsprint was yellowed and frail. It was dated 1924.

MADMAN MASSACRES SEVEN IN DANISH SEMINARY

Last weekend in the small, picturesque, and currently snow-covered, town of Grena in Denmark occurred the tragic and apparently motiveless murder of seven innocent schoolboys. One of their class-mates, brandishing a kitchen knife, attacked the boys in the dormitory of Grena's most prestigious educational establishment. Before he was finally overpowered, seven of those who should have been his friends lay on their bloodied beds, deprived of life. The only motive for his crimes that the insane young man offered was that "they were laughing at my foot". The murderer, who is likely to spend the rest of his life in a secure institution was named Sven
Cont. Pg. 17

But of "Pg. 17", needless to say, there was no sign.

"That's the link," Maria burst out in an excited whisper. "It must be. The Puzzels *did* survive. Sonia and Gervaise escaped back to Denmark, which is where she'd come from originally. Randers – wasn't that the name of the town where she was supposed to have killed her parents?"

"Is that in Denmark?" asked Jack, whose education had not been as thorough as that of the bishop and actress's daughter.

"Yes. A bit north of Arhus. *And*," she continued with mounting animation, "not far from Grena."

"Ah," said Jack. "So if Sonia and Gervaise resettled in that area . . ."

"Well, this Sven must have been a descendant of theirs . . ."

"Bearing the 'Puzzel Peculiaritie' . . ."

"The foot deformity, of course! That must have been what the other boys laughed at . . ."

"Yes, and he must have inherited the genetic homicidal tendencies from Sonia Puzzel . . ."

"Look!" Maria pointed triumphantly at the cutting. "It was snowing when the attack took place! The dreadful psychological effects of Gervaise's exposure to the snow must have been carried down through the generations too."

"Hm. If only we had 'Pg. 17', the continuation of this cutting . . . If only we had the schoolboy murderer's surname . . ."

"I'd put money on the fact that it's 'Altmidson'," Maria pronounced with unshakeable conviction.

"No, love, we can't be absolutely sure of that yet. There may be other people here with Danish connections. Didn't you hear Barbara Hood saying that Bob's family originated in Scandinavia? And we don't know what country Count Leontchy comes from. It could even be that –"

"Oh, for heaven's sake, Jack! It must be him! It must be Anders!"

"I agree it's possible, but –"

"Yes, I know all about your professional caution and your unwillingness to jump to conclusions and the rest of it, but this is serious. We can't afford to wait till we're absolutely certain. If we confront him now, there's a chance that we can stop another murder!"

Jack Tarrant still wasn't totally convinced, but he nodded. "All right. We should at least talk to him."

And so they would have done – had they been able to find him.

They went first to the Hunters' Bar, where some of the guests were still drinking the tea which the chef had so recently announced, but he wasn't there.

They checked the other public areas and Maria even slipped into the kitchen, but there was no sign of him.

They met Nerys by Reception and asked if she had seen him. She hadn't, but she generously offered to try the intercom to his room (which was battery-operated and so unaffected by the power cut), but its buzzing evinced no reply.

It seemed that Anders Altmidson was in hiding.

And the thought of the new horrors that the crazed Puzzel heir might be organising from his hiding-place put ice in the blood of Jack Tarrant and Maria Lethbury.

There was a rather poor turn-out for the advertised "Party Games" at 8.30 p.m. Some of the guests were still apparently sleeping off the effects of their lunch, while others had maybe decided that "Party Games" were not for them.

Bob and Barbara Hood were there, eager not to miss anything that might possibly constitute part of a traditional English Christmas. Alexander Honeycutt was there, hoping for a bit of fun to leaven the adult conversation that surrounded him. Count Leo Leontchy was there, smiling enigmatically, giving, as usual, no clue to his motivations.

Jack Tarrant and Maria Lethbury were there, because the "Party Games" were advertised on the brochure and they had seen how closely their quarry tied his surprises to the scheduled events in the Christmas Break programme.

Celia Tranmere and Peggy Smith-Brously were also on hand, though not actually in the entrance hall where the games were supposed to be taking place. They had adjourned to the Hunters' Bar, where Jan Stout served them drinks. Since they had found a backgammon board on the bar, they started a desultory game, announcing that they'd come back to the hall if the "Party Games" proved to be irresistible.

The chances of this happening were slender, chiefly because there was no one to run them. Among the many duties which Trentham Metcalfe had agreed (for a not insubstantial fee) to undertake over the holiday at Puzzel Manor was acting as Master of these particular Revels.

At the original interview he had assured the Stouts that he was an expert at "Charades" and "Murder in the Dark", that his organisation of "Postman's Knock" and "Musical Chairs" had never been bettered, and that no one had ever run a more hilarious session of "Clumps" or "Are You There, Moriarty?"

Now all these claims may have been true, but the fact was that, at the moment he was meant to be demonstrating his skills, Trentham Metcalfe presumably lay snoring in his room, dead to the world.

And, after the Dickens debacle, the Stouts did not risk waking him. They were not afraid that he would be unwilling to fulfil his contractual duties. (He was, after all, as he kept telling them, an old pro who had never been known to miss a performance.) But they were worried about the kind of performance he might turn in, and its potential for upsetting their guests. It was deemed more prudent, therefore, to let him sleep.

Roddy Stout appointed himself to step into the jollity breach, but, though there was no questioning his willingness, he patently had no aptitude for the task.

For a start, he didn't seem to know the rules of any of the games, and kept consulting the sheaf of notes on his lap. These were presumably written by Trentham Metcalfe, because the hotel proprietor had great difficulty in deciphering the unfamiliar handwriting.

"Now, how about starting off with a jolly round of 'Are You There, Moriarty?'" he began tentatively. "All we need for this is a rolled-up newspaper and a . . ." he screwed up his eyes as he looked at the notes – "a bill-fold . . . ?"

"A blindfold," Alexander Honeycutt rather testily corrected him.

"Oh, right. Now I'm sure I can go and find a newspaper and a scarf or something . . ."

"Would it not be better," Count Leo Leontchy suggested politely, "for us to play a game for which we have the requisite equipment already here?"

"Yes, certainly, if you . . . How about 'Musical Chairs'? We've got plenty of chairs here."

"But you haven't got any music," said Alexander Honeycutt grumpily, "just as you haven't got any television, because you haven't got any power."

"Oh, that's true," Roddy Stout agreed. "Well, maybe someone's got a battery cassette player or . . ." He riffled through the sheets of notes. "Perhaps we should play something else. "'Clumps' . . . ?" he offered hopefully.

"Now I don't know that game," said Bob Hood.

"Never heard of it," said Barbara Hood. "'Clumps' – what a curious name. How do you play it?"

"Well, erm . . ." Another frantic scramble through the notes. "Well, erm, it seems you have two teams and, er, well, the aim of the game seems to be . . . um . . ."

Roddy Stout floundered on for a few more minutes, before Count Leontchy said, if they would excuse him, he thought he might go and have a drink. Bob and Barbara Hood speedily came round to the view that a drink was at least as traditionally English as "Party Games", and Alexander Honeycutt wandered off soon after, grumbling about being stuck for Christmas in a hotel that didn't even have a working television.

Roddy Stout looked apologetically at Jack and Maria. "Oh. Well, if people don't want to play games, you can't make them. Much better to just let people do what they want, rather than force things on them, don't you think? Our guests are all meant to be on holiday, after all."

"Yes. Mr Stout, you remember the body we found in the chapel?"

"Yes, of course." He put the notes down on a table beside him and looked nervously at his watch. "Good heavens, is that the time? Sorry, couple of things I have to check through with Nerys." And he had scuttled out of the room before

Solve this quickly and you might save the answer! (Reception had a list of names to choose from.) Otherwise, it's one in the eye for you, Jack Tarrant!

either of them could say another word.

Jack moved his wheelchair swiftly forward and picked up the "Party Games" notes.

"Do you think there might be . . . ?"

"I think there well might be, Maria. Ah." He extracted a sheet from the pile. "Look, once again we see the calling card."

"Which segment of the shield is that?"

"It's – good heavens, it's the one that comes directly after 'Who Will Be The Next Victim?' So there's a very strong chance that the answer will be the victim's name. Yes, and the message he's written supports that."

They both stared at the strange design on the page.

"I think it could be an anagram," said Jack.

"What, and the answer's a name?"

"I should think so. 'Reception had a list of names to choose from' . . . ? Presumably that means the names of the guests in the Visitors' Book . . . ?"

"Yes." Maria's smooth brow furrowed as she looked at the puzzle. "I can't make any of the guests' names out of . . ." She stopped suddenly and looked at Jack. "Hey, I just had a thought . . ."

"What?"

"That word 'Reception' could mean something else. Think, Jack, think. What was the first event on the programme for this Christmas Break?"

"The 'Ice-breaking Reception'."

"Exactly. Where we were all supposed to be given silly names . . ."

"Yes." Jack Tarrant's eye glinted feverishly. "And there was a list of which name was supposed to go with which person. Didn't you pick up that list?"

"Yes, I did. It's in the bedroom."

"Come on then!"

Back in the Yellow Room, Maria Lethbury found the relevant scrap of paper and spread it out on the fireside table. Jack had paper and pencils ready and they started to work out the anagram.

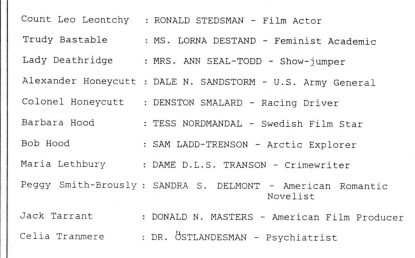

```
Count Leo Leontchy    : RONALD STEDSMAN - Film Actor

Trudy Bastable        : MS. LORNA DESTAND - Feminist Academic

Lady Deathridge       : MRS. ANN SEAL-TODD - Show-jumper

Alexander Honeycutt : DALE N. SANDSTORM - U.S. Army General

Colonel Honeycutt     : DENSTON SMALARD - Racing Driver

Barbara Hood          : TESS NORDMANDAL - Swedish Film Star

Bob Hood              : SAM LADD-TRENSON - Arctic Explorer

Maria Lethbury        : DAME D.L.S. TRANSON - Crimewriter

Peggy Smith-Brously : SANDRA S. DELMONT - American Romantic
                                          Novelist

Jack Tarrant          : DONALD N. MASTERS - American Film Producer

Celia Tranmere        : DR. ÖSTLANDESMAN - Psychiatrist
```

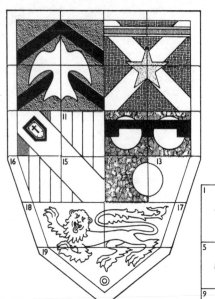

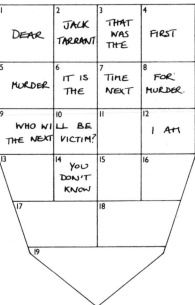

1 DEAR	2 JACK TARRANT	3 THAT WAS THE	4 FIRST
5 MURDER	6 IT IS THE	7 TIME NEXT	8 FOR MURDER.
9 WHO WILL BE THE NEXT	10 VICTIM?	11	12 I AM
13	14 YOU DON'T KNOW	15	16
17		18	
19			

THIS IS HOW JACK AND MARIA SOLVED THE NINTH PUZZLE:

Quickly realising that the large numbers could only be line references, and the small numbers word references within those lines, all they had to do to find the answer was to count down to the relevant lines and across to the relevant words.

ELEVEN

CHRISTMAS DAY – 10.30 P.M. "MURDER IN THE DARK", ETC.

"It must be Lady Deathridge!" shouted Maria. "All of the letters are in 'MRS. ANN SEAL-TODD'!"

But at the same moment, Jack Tarrant cried, "God, he's a monster. It's the boy – Alexander! 'DALE N. SANDSTORM''s the anagram!"

They looked at each other for a perplexed moment, then turned back to the sheet and checked their answers.

"Oh, no, I don't believe it," Jack groaned.

"So it could be either of them . . ." Maria's face clouded. "Oh no, or it could be *both*!"

"I don't think so." Jack shook his head grimly. "The bastard's playing with us again. I don't think he's telling us anything – just that *one* of the guests is about to be murdered. And while that murder's quite possibly taking place, we're stuck here playing fatuous word games!"

"What, you mean that *all* these names . . . ?"

"I think so. We'd better check, but I think we'll find they're all anagrams of each other."

They checked, and it didn't take long to find out that Jack had been right.

121

"So, what was that in aid of? Just sheer viciousness on his part?"

"Perhaps, Maria. I wonder . . . I mean I'm sure the viciousness was part of it. And he wanted to waste our time, but . . ." Contemplatively, he rubbed the bristles on his chin. "The puzzle must have an answer, though. I mean, he did put in a bit of the coat of arms, after all. And there must be a single correct solution to fill in on the grid – he wouldn't leave it as a multiple choice. His mind doesn't work like that. He likes everything neat and tidy, no loose ends. He has the obsessive perfectionism of the psychopath."

"Well, maybe there's another clue in the original piece of paper . . ." Maria took the "DEAD MORTAL" sheet and studied it. "Maybe we did misinterpret 'Reception' . . . Maybe it *did* mean the Reception of the hotel . . ."

"Yes, but if it was the Visitors' Book, we've got the list of the guests' names and none of them fits the anagram."

"No, but there might be other lists at Reception . . . Lists of staff . . . ? Lists of people living in Puzzel Moultby . . . ?"

"Hm." Jack also stared at the frustrating sheet of paper.

"Maybe we were wrong about it being an anagram . . . ?"

"Maybe. I don't know, Maria. I'm sure the clue is here. There's something on this piece of paper that should point us in the right direction. Every other puzzle he's done has followed a kind of logic."

"Pretty weird logic some of the time. Strange, twisted Scandinavian logic."

Jack looked up at her. "You're absolutely convinced it's Anders?"

"Well, who else can it be? If he's inherited all the Puzzel genes, he's certainly a psychopath. And if Anton arrived with the intention of blackmailing his brother or contesting his inheritance, then Anders has a motive that would work even for someone who wasn't a psychopath."

"Yes. It is beginning to look that way, isn't it?"

"Good heavens." She gaped in mock-amazement. "Am I witnessing that unprecedented phenomenon, the great Jack Tarrant – Mr Pussyfoot himself – actually leaping to a conclusion?"

"No, Maria, not quite. You are witnessing him homing in on a possibility, though."

"Oh, well, I'll have to be content with that for the time being."

Jack grinned and returned his attention to the puzzle. "Why does he say it'd be 'one in the eye' for me . . . ? Is that a threat? Am I about to be shot in the eye? Maybe *I'm* the next victim . . ."

"Oh, Jack!" She clasped her arms round his shoulders.

"Don't worry. He's not going to get me that easily. I'll be ready for him." Jack Tarrant became thoughtful again and drummed his fingertips on the arm of his wheelchair as he repeated, "'One in the eye', 'one in the eye', 'one in the –' Oh, my God!"

He pointed to the sheet of paper. "Look, Maria, look!"

"What am I meant to be looking at?"

"The shape that the puzzle's in! Don't you see? It's an –"

"An 'I'!"

"Exactly. That's the meaning of 'one in the I'!"

"So if we try the anagram with the original letters *plus* an 'I', we get . . . ?"

"Oh, no!" Jack Tarrant's hands flew to the wheels of his chair. "Quick, Maria, quick! We might still get there in time to stop him!"

They didn't.

As they burst into the kitchen, they saw Anders Altmidson lying spreadeagled on the table. From his chest protruded the black haft of a large Sabatier kitchen knife. Blood was still spreading outwards from the wound across the virgin white of the chef's jacket, but he was very still.

"No!" Maria murmured, as Jack wheeled himself towards the body.

"Oh, my God!"

They both turned at the sound of a voice behind them. Roddy Stout stood there, his eyes popping out of his florid face. He wrung his hands. "Not another one!"

"Yes, Mr Stout, another one." Jack Tarrant looked at the hotelier coldly. "And are you proposing to keep this death secret from your guests as well?"

"Well, I –"

"What the devil's going on?" Colonel Honeycutt had appeared in the doorway behind Roddy. "Mr Stout, heard you cry out and . . ." He became aware of the body on the table. "I say. Bad show. How on earth did that happen?"

"We don't know yet, but we're –"

Jack was interrupted by a blood-curdling scream from somewhere in the body of the hotel. He and Maria rushed instantly out of the kitchen to the source of the sound.

They found it in the Hunters' Bar. A sobbing Trudy Bastable was alone in the room, cowering against the counter. The tears that poured down her face glinted in the candlelight.

Maria Lethbury immediately put her arms around the terrified woman and murmured words of comfort. Gradually, the hysterics subsided.

"What was it? What happened?" asked Jack with gentle firmness.

Trudy Bastable shuddered as she replied, the words dragged painfully from deep within her. "I'd just come down to pick up Lady Deathridge's handbag. She'd left it earlier and I saw – I saw . . ."

Tears threatened again, but Jack had not forgotten his police interrogation skills. "Yes?" he said patiently. "Don't rush. Just tell me in your own time."

"I saw . . . I saw someone dressed in the Santa Claus suit . . ."

"Who? Was it Trentham Metcalfe?"

"I don't know. I couldn't see the face. He had the beard on, and the hood was pulled forward. But . . . but . . . but . . ."

"Yes?"

"He was holding up a knife – a big kitchen knife. And it was dripping with blood!"

"Look, you just calm down. Maria, perhaps Trudy'd like a brandy? That might help."

"Well, I don't usually drink much and . . ."

But when Maria went behind the counter and poured a large balloon of Courvoisier, Trudy Bastable did not refuse it.

"This figure you saw . . ." Jack began casually once the first

124

large gulp had gone down, "which way was it going?"

"I saw it in the hall. It seemed to have come from . . . well, from the direction of the kitchen, I suppose . . . and then it went off up the stairs."

"I see."

"It was horrible!"

"Now, don't you worry about it," Jack reassured her, before the tears could start up again. "Maybe it was a trick of the light or someone playing a practical joke or –"

"But it looked completely real," the frightened woman protested.

"I think you should just get to bed. Put it out of your mind. You'll feel better after a good night's sleep."

"Well . . ."

"Will you sleep? Have you got something you can take?" asked Maria.

"Yes. Yes, I've got some pills. But don't you think I should really – ?"

"I think all you should do is get to bed." Jack spoke softly, but there was no doubt that his words were an order.

She made no further attempt to argue, but let Maria lead her, sobbing softly, across the hall and up the stairs.

Jack pursed his lips and looked around the bar. He was about to go back to investigate the murder scene in the kitchen, when he saw the backgammon board on which Celia Tranmere and Peggy Smith-Brously had been playing earlier in the evening.

The more he looked at it, the odder it seemed.

For a start, one side had far more counters than it should.

Then he noticed, on the dividing "bar" of the board, a strange design. It was part of the Puzzel coat of arms.

He looked closely at the game, and racked his memory for the rules of backgammon.

Then he remembered the directions in which the white and black counters have to move.

He took a piece of paper and a pencil and tried a few permutations. None of them worked.

Controlling his frustration, Jack Tarrant studied the board

again. He looked at the twelve "points" on each side, and he looked at the "bar". After a little while, he wrote down the three-word answer to the eleventh Puzzel Manor puzzle.

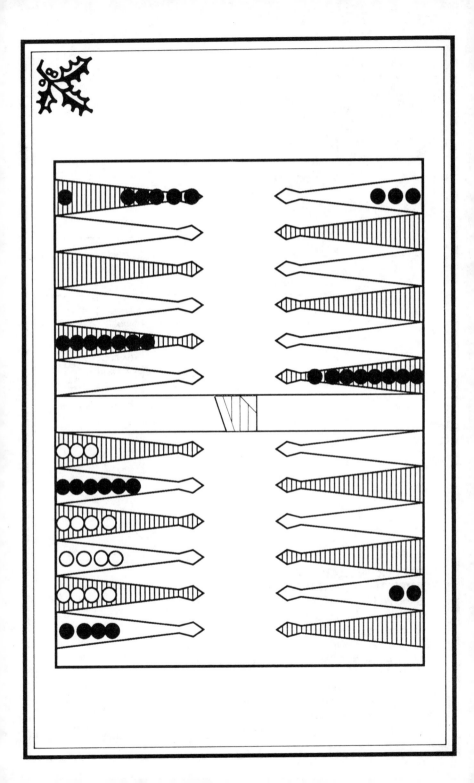

1 DEAR	2 JACK TARRANT	3 THAT WAS THE	4 FIRST
5 MURDER	6 IT IS THE	7 TIME NEXT	8 FOR MURDER.
9 WHO WILL BE THE NEXT	10 VICTIM?	11 ANDERS ALTMIDSON	12 I AM
13	14 YOU DON'T KNOW	15	16
17		18	
19			

THIS IS HOW JACK AND MARIA
SOLVED THE TENTH PUZZLE:

As indicated in the previous chapter, Jack and
Maria fell into the murderer's trap and tried to work
out anagrams of the names used at the Ice-Breaking
Reception. And, sure enough, they found that all the
names were anagrams of each other, as well as of
the letters from "DEAD MORTAL NS NS". It was
only when they understood the "one in the eye" clue
that they looked again at the shape in which the
other letters were set, added an "I" to the pool and
found the answer - though, apparently, too late!

TWELVE

CHRISTMAS DAY – 11.00 P.M. CHRISTMAS CAKE

Jack Tarrant seethed with fury when he had worked out the puzzle. He was being given so little. He was like a boxer kept at arm's length until his opponent chose to attack. And his opponent seemed to have all the time in the world to pick where he wanted to place his shots. The second murder had been an undoubted body-blow, and Jack had a nasty feeling that the murderer was squaring up for a knockout.

The second murder also threw into disarray all Jack's previous thinking about the case. Though professional caution kept him from Maria's positive assertions, he had been moving closer and closer to the view that Anders Altmidson had killed his brother Anton and was the brains behind all the macabre games at Puzzel Manor. But the chef's death completely invalidated that theory, and left the identity of the teasing psychopath once again wide open.

At least this time Jack was determined to make a proper investigation of the scene of the crime. Roddy Stout might not have allowed one murder to ruffle the elegant surface of his precious Christmas Break, but it was going to be very hard to keep two quiet. Apart from anything else, one of the guests,

Colonel Honeycutt, had seen the second victim, and Jack couldn't envisage the Colonel having the will or imagination to subscribe to the hotelier's cover-up policy.

He heard the two of them arguing on just this point, as he propelled his wheelchair towards the kitchen door.

"No, murders have to be investigated," Colonel Honeycutt was insisting. "Can't have dead bodies lying around the place. Police job."

"I fully agree," said Roddy Stout, "but how do we contact the police? The phone lines are down, no one can get out of the hotel . . ."

"We don't *know* that. Nobody's tried very hard to get out, have they? Padre chappie – Reverend Thing – managed to make it across to his place."

"But his phone's not working either."

"Not my point. Mean if someone can get that far, can maybe get a lot further."

"The snow's very deep," Roddy Stout objected. "A lot of drifts, and this is pretty treacherous country. I wouldn't fancy trying to get anywhere in that lot."

"Some things just have to be done. In this case, police need to be summoned. Got helicopters, that kind of stuff. They could get out here."

"Only if they knew they were needed out here. And I don't see how we're going to tell them."

Roddy managed to sound both helpless and triumphant. So long as the weather held, he would get through his full Christmas programme. And if they'd had their full programme, then the guests couldn't ask for their money back. Roddy Stout was a man for whom profit came first, with justice a long way behind.

"And of what possible benefit," he asked, adding to his argument, "could it be for us to tell the rest of the guests what has happened? It would only cause wholesale panic. It's my job as an hotelier," he concluded righteously, "to ensure that my guests are disrupted as little as possible."

"I agree that we don't want the guests upset," said Jack, who had just joined them, "but I also agree with Colonel Honeycutt that we must somehow let the police know what's happened."

"But *how*?" Roddy Stout spread his hands wide in gleeful impotence.

"I'll go and tell them," said the Colonel decisively. "I've been trained for most conditions. Sure a bit of snow's not going to stop me. I'll take my boy Alexander along. Better with two in these situations."

"I think you're taking a big risk. The hotel's insurance wouldn't cover you for an accident outside the grounds."

But Colonel Honeycutt was not to be deflected by Roddy Stout's arguments. "No, mind made up. Going out there. Fetch police. They'll nail the swine who's done this." He turned suddenly to Jack. "You used to be a copper, didn't you, Tarrant?"

"Yes."

"Don't you think what I'm suggesting's the right thing?"

"Certainly. The sooner we get the professionals in investigating this, the sooner we can remove the risk of more murders."

He said it automatically, but within Jack Tarrant was a niggling disappointment. He hadn't admitted to himself how much he wanted to be the one who solved the case. The fact that he had been so directly addressed by the killer, the fact that at times the whole scenario seemed to come down to a personal battle of wits between the two of them, made him want desperately to play the game through. And to end up the winner.

But Colonel Honeycutt was right. They should make contact with the police. Indeed, had the telephones been working, that would have been Jack Tarrant's first reaction after the discovery of the body in the Puzzel chapel. It was only the mounting claustrophobia of the murderer's fiendish game-plan that had made him so far forget his professional standards as even to contemplate an amateur solution.

Because, as he had once again painfully to remind himself, that's what he was – an amateur. Jack Tarrant's career as a Scotland Yard detective was over. He should stand back gracefully and make room for the professionals.

"Right. I'll go and wake the boy. Sooner we get off, the better."

Colonel Honeycutt started towards the hall, then stopped. "Better lock the kitchen, Stout. Don't want anyone going in there, getting a nasty shock, do we?"

"Before it's locked," said Jack coolly, "I'd like to have a look round."

"What the devil for?"

"As you said, Colonel, I used to be a policeman. Homicide detective, as it happens. If I have a look round the scene of the crime, I might find some clues to the murderer's identity."

"Yes. Equally, Tarrant, if you yourself had killed the poor bastard, you might go in there and *remove* some clues to the murderer's identity."

"I can assure you, Colonel, that –"

"Sorry, Tarrant. All suspects, I'm afraid. Every one of us. Safer if we lock the kitchen door till the police come."

"But how're we going to manage to cook breakfast tomorrow morning?" asked Roddy Stout with an hotelier's professional anxiety.

"Oh yes, could be tricky without a chef, couldn't it?"

"No, that's all right. Jan's an excellent cook. Wasn't what I meant. I meant how're we going to do it if the kitchen's still locked and has a corpse inside it?"

"Bit of luck, Alexander and I'll be back with the police before that becomes a problem."

"Maybe, but –"

"No argument about it. Right thing to do. I'll go and wake the boy now. We'll get going quickly as possible."

And Colonel Honeycutt marched off towards the stairs.

Jack Tarrant watched with annoyance as Roddy Stout locked the kitchen door. Not of course that that would keep him out. Thirty seconds with his picklock and he'd be inside. No, the annoying thing was that his scene of the crime investigation would have to wait until after everyone had gone to bed.

Never mind. He'd get in there. And he felt certain that a detailed inspection of the kitchen would yield some clue to the murderer's identity.

Because Jack Tarrant felt more determined than ever that he was going to catch the killer. And, though he wouldn't have voiced the thought, even to himself, what he meant was "catch the killer before the police do".

In the Yellow Room Jack looked yet again at the slowly filling shield-shaped grid of messages from his antagonist. Fourteen segments filled, five remaining. And all the information he had more or less useless.

The killer was torturing him, teasing him, playing him along, supremely confident that his own intellect was superior to that of Jack Tarrant. The only solid fact that the puzzles had provided was the name of the second victim, "Anders Altmidson". And the murderer had ensured that, by the time Jack got to that information, it would be too late for him to use it.

No, the important facts were still to come. Jack felt sure that the final segment, the triangle at the bottom of the shield, was destined eventually to contain the killer's name. It would be typical of the arrogance and exhibitionism demonstrated in all the other puzzles.

But equally Jack felt certain that the killer did not intend his identity to be known until he had safely escaped. And how many more outrages did he plan to commit before that moment arrived?

The door opened and Jack looked up from the grid as Maria entered.

"Trudy's safely tucked up in bed. She took a couple of pills and seemed to have calmed down quite a bit."

"Good."

"Just hope Lady Deathridge doesn't wake in the night and demand to be waited on. The old bat really does treat that poor woman like rubbish."

"Lady Deathridge treats everyone like rubbish, as far as I can tell."

"Mm. I was a long time upstairs, wasn't I?" Maria observed mischievously.

"I assumed Trudy took a long time to settle."

"Not that long."

"So what have you been up to?"

"Well, I thought about what she said she saw . . . you know, what made her scream . . . ?"

"Mm."

"So I thought I might investigate where the Santa Claus outfit was."

"Sensible girl. And . . . ?"

"*And* I found the beard on the floor, and the coat all crumpled up on a chair, just as if it had been thrown down, in the bedroom belonging to . . . ?"

He looked at her quizzically, playing along with her histrionics.

". . . Trentham Metcalfe," she concluded.

"Very interesting."

"What is more, although the Santa Claus outfit was there, Trentham Metcalfe wasn't."

"Ah. Any sign of the bloody kitchen knife Trudy Bastable saw?"

"No. No sign of bloodstains on the coat either."

"Well, well, well . . ."

"One of the oldest – and easiest – tricks in the book, pretending to be drunk."

"Certainly."

"Particularly easy for an actor. And he arrived at Puzzel Manor earlier than most of the guests, so he had time to set things up . . ."

"That's true, too."

"And quite a lot of the puzzles have been found in things that Trentham handled. The Ghost Story book . . . the copy of *Pickwick Papers* . . . the list of names at the Ice-breaking Reception –"

"Though that last one turned out to be a red herring."

"Yes, but you could say it was he who fed us the red herring."

Jack nodded, deep in thought, then moved his head sharply at a sound from outside the window. Maria moved swiftly across and drew the curtain back an inch. Jack wheeled himself alongside her.

It had started to snow again, smaller flakes now, but steady and relentless. Enough light spilled from the windows at the front of Puzzel Manor for them to see, close to, Alexander Honeycutt's snowman, and, beyond it, the swaddled shapes of the boy himself and his father, as they set out across the deep-pile carpet of snow towards the distant yew tree that marked the manor's main gates.

Colonel Honeycutt pointed their way with a strong torchbeam, and both carried sticks, which they certainly needed to maintain balance. Their progress forward was agonisingly slow. Each footfall sank down into the whiteness, up to the top of his thigh in Alexander's case, and then each leg had to be dragged up for the next step forward.

"Going to be some time before they make contact with the police," murmured Jack.

"Still, it's good that at last someone's *trying* to make contact with the police. Means there's a chance that this nightmare will be over that much sooner."

"Yes, Maria. Yes . . ."

And in his voice there was a note almost of wistfulness.

For the second night in a row, Jack Tarrant and Maria Lethbury moved noiselessly along the dark corridors of Puzzel Manor. This time the picklock was used in the kitchen rather than the ice-house keyhole.

As the door gave inwards, Maria shone her torch on to the table in the centre of the room.

Nothing.

The body of Anders Altmidson had disappeared.

They moved forward as one. Only a few drops of bright red on the scrubbed pine surface bore witness to the fact that a murder victim had lain there a few hours before.

There was nothing else unexpected on the tabletop. A flour-dusted chopping board, a couple of saucepans, an eggwhisk, some spoons, butter rigid in a dish, a tray of eggs, a recipe book open in a transparent plastic stand. It looked as if the chef's life had been cut short in mid-creation.

Maria moved rapidly round the room, checking the cupboards and other potential hiding-places, but there was no body. She turned the torch on Jack's face.

135

"Ice-house?"

He nodded.

The picklock did its stuff, and they were once more in the insulated deadness of the ice-house. Anton's body was still fixed in the cot, a grotesque parody of infancy.

Maria's torchbeam invaded all the nooks and crannies of the place, but there was no second body. Thoughtfully, they returned to the kitchen.

Jack wheeled himself close to the table and scrutinised the glistening droplets on the wood.

"Too bright for arterial blood," he said. "Anyway, blood would have dried and gone brown by now."

He reached a finger forward and touched at one of the spots. The redness stuck tackily to his fingertip. He moved it to his nose and sniffed.

"Paint. Red paint."

"You mean it's a double bluff? He's not dead?"

"Looks that way. Damn! If only I'd had a chance to look closely at the body when we first saw it."

"It was Roddy coming in that stopped us."

"Yes. Yes, so it was . . ." He was thoughtful for a moment. "Could you shine the torch on the table?"

"Are you expecting another message?"

"It would fit in with his usual style, wouldn't it? Every other time he's pulled one of his coups, he's had a little crow about it and left us a calling card."

"I notice you're no longer saying 'or she', Jack . . ."

"No, well, I think this has rather narrowed the options. Anders was high on our list of suspects before. Now he's faked his own death, he's more or less admitting that it's him."

"So why *did* he fake his own death? Were we not meant to find out that the body'd gone?"

"No, everything that's happened to us since we arrived at Puzzel Manor has been *meant*. He's just playing on our nerves."

Maria's scanning torchbeam stopped on the open recipe book. Its cover was towards them, an old, blotched paper binding on which had been written in an ancient hand: *Household Receipts of Puzzel Manor.*

They moved round to look at the opened pages, through the anti-splash plastic of the modern stand.

"Look!" said Maria. "On the right-hand side. There's the bit of the coat of arms."

"Yes."

They both studied the grubby page, on which an antique recipe had been scrawled in faded sepia ink.

"Well, it's nonsense, no question about that," Maria announced. "You couldn't begin to cook that if you tried."

"Yes, the words are nonsense, but there's something in it that isn't nonsense. What's 'saltire'? Is it an old word for 'salt'?"

"No, Jack."

"A version of 'satire'?"

"No."

"Well, come on, Maria," he said rather testily. "Let me have the benefit of all that education the bishop and actress paid for."

She put on the prim expression of a class knowall. "A 'saltire' is an heraldic term."

"Oh. Well, what do you know? Afraid you don't get to do much on heraldry at Police College."

"A 'saltire' is an 'ordinary'."

"Thanks a bundle. You'll have to give me more than that."

So she told him what it was. "Like St Andrew's," she concluded. "There's one on the Puzzel coat of arms."

"Oh yes, I see."

He looked again at the recipe for "Elephant Pie".

Then, as comprehension dawned, all the colour left his face and his mouth began to tremble uncontrollably.

"Oh, no!" Jack Tarrant gasped. "Oh, no! NO!!!"

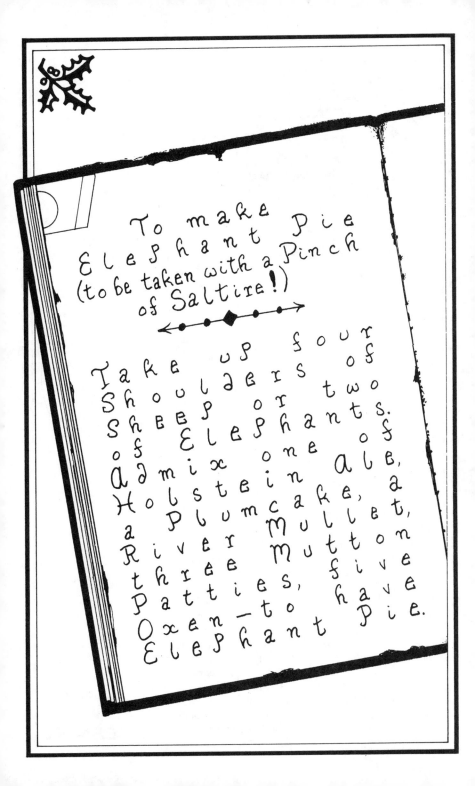

To make
Elephant Pie
(to be taken with a Pinch
of Saltire!)

Take up four
Shoulders of
Sheep or two
of Elephants.
Admix one of
Holstein Ale,
a Plumcake, at,
River Mullet,
three Mutton
Patties, five
Oxen—to have
Elephant Pie.

1 DEAR	2 JACK TARRANT	3 THAT WAS THE	4 FIRST
5 MURDER	6 IT IS THE	7 TIME NEXT	8 FOR MURDER.
9 WHO WILL BE THE NEXT VICTIM?	10	11 ANDERS ALTHIDSON	12 I AM
13	14 YOU DON'T KNOW	15	16 MY NAME IS.
17	18		
19			

THIS IS HOW JACK
SOLVED THE ELEVENTH PUZZLE:

Knowing that each side at backgammon has fifteen counters, he quickly saw that there were too many blacks on the board. He then noticed that the twelve "points" or spikes on each side, plus one space each side for the "bar" in the middle, made the significant total of twenty-six. So, going in the direction that the black counters have to move to reach the black "inner table" in backgammon, he assigned a letter of the alphabet to each "point" and the two "bar" spaces. To find the sequence of the resulting letters, he had noticed that the black counters were clustered in groups of 1, 2, 3 and so on up to 8 (with both 1 and 5 on the same point). In this way he was able to find the three-word answer.

THIRTEEN

BOXING DAY – 3.00 A.M. NIGHTCAP

"What is it?" asked Maria.

"Nothing. Nothing." Instinctively, Jack Tarrant's hands had covered the Elephant Pie recipe.

"No, it is something. And I have to know too, Jack. Come on, we're in this together. We're in everything together, Jack."

Gently, but firmly, her strong fingers prised his off the page. She looked down at the recipe for a moment, then gave a grim flick of her head as understanding came. "I see."

"It's what I've been afraid of from the start." Jack's shoulders seemed to shrink as he slumped in the wheelchair. "There's nothing we can do. We're at his mercy. He's been picking his moments all along. Now we just have to wait till he chooses his final moment – and his final outrage."

"Nonsense!" The bishop had passed on to his daughter all the vigour of his own "Muscular Christianity". Maria's red hair glistened defiantly in the torchlight as she tossed her head. "We're at least equal to him."

"We haven't been so far. He's dictated the timing of the whole campaign. Every decision we've made has been forced on us."

"Then it's about time we changed all that. About time we started to take the initiative."

"Yes, but how? He seems to have complete control of Puzzel

Manor – setting up clues, moving bodies at will inside the house – and probably outside."

"Mm. He does seem very efficient . . . and you know what that suggests to me, Jack . . . ?"

"What?"

"That he's not working on his own."

"An accomplice?"

"Make a lot of the logistics easier, wouldn't it? One causes a distraction while the other sets out a puzzle, that kind of thing . . . "

"You could be right."

"Anyway, our task is very straightforward – all we've got to do is to find Anders and lock him up before he can commit another crime."

"You make it sound so easy."

"It is," she asserted with a breezy confidence whose basis neither of them would have liked to investigate. "And at least we now do know who we're looking for. It all makes sense. Anders Altmidson had inherited the psychopathic tendencies of the Puzzel family; he had reasons of blackmail to kill his brother Anton; and his diatribe against the female executives who used to come to his restaurant gives a kind of perverted motivation for 'The Executive Exterminator''s crimes."

Jack caught the glint of her teeth in the torchlight as Maria grinned at him. "You realise what, Jack? You now have the opportunity for total revenge. When you get him, you'll be tying up not only the Puzzel Manor murder, but all the others as well."

"So long as he doesn't get me first . . ." Then, with sudden determination, Jack Tarrant banished his defeatism. "But you're right – I won't let him! Sorry about my little lapse there. It's just the shock. I went all feeble and –"

"You don't have to apologise to me, Jack. I understand how much the whole business means to you . . . being stuck in the wheelchair, your sense of having failed . . . everything . . ."

"Thanks." He clasped her hand on his shoulder for a moment; then he looked pensive. "Just had a thought . . ."

"Mm?"

142

"Your idea of an accomplice – I like that. And I think I can cast the part perfectly."

"Who?"

"A very versatile actor who can play all kinds of different roles."

"Trentham Metcalfe?"

"Yes. Think about it. Think about the timing of when we found Anders' body. We came in here, just had time to take in what appeared to be a murder, and then were distracted by Trudy Bastable's scream . . ."

"So Trentham was waiting for his cue? Waiting till he saw us go into the kitchen, then he manifested himself to scare the wits out of Trudy?"

"That would fit the facts, wouldn't it? Because, when you think about it, there was something pretty odd about what she saw."

Maria's mind was once again moving as quickly as his. "The bloodstained knife!"

"Yes. The only bloodstained knife around was the one stuck into Anders Altmidson's chest – which we now know was just a set-up . . ."

"So Trentham was only carrying one to look frightening – to prompt the reaction from Trudy?"

"Exactly. What's the time?"

Maria turned the torch on to her wristwatch. "Nearly three."

"Right." Jack Tarrant started to wheel himself out of the kitchen. One could not have believed that this was the same man who had so recently succumbed to impotent despair. "Back to the Yellow Room. We're going to work out a plan of campaign. We're going to start taking the initiative now. You were right, Maria. There's no question about it – we're going to nail the bastard!"

It was as they passed the Reception desk that they heard the click. It seemed to come from the inner office.

Both froze. Then the click was repeated. And again.

Maria grabbed at the handles of Jack's wheelchair and pushed him forward to the office door. As she did so, both seemed to hear a slight rustle from the landing above them.

Jack and Maria froze again, but the rustle was not repeated.

They went through into the office and closed the door. The click sounded louder.

Maria's torchbeam traced it to the fax machine. "As I thought," she said in a triumphant whisper.

"What? I'm not with you."

"Listen." As Maria spoke, she was fumbling with the wiring behind the fax. "The main phone line to Puzzel Manor has been down since Christmas Eve, and everyone's assumed that that's because all the phone lines in the Puzzel Moultby area are down. Then when the electricity failed, the fax power obviously went off too. But nobody thought actually to check the fax *line* . . ."

"Which would, of course, be separate."

"Yes. And I think this clicking is someone trying to get through on the fax line."

"But they can't send a fax when the power's down."

"No. But a fax line is no different from an ordinary phone line, so if I take out the fax connection and plug in the ordinary phone to the socket . . . like *so*, then –"

She was instantly rewarded by a ping from the telephone, which would have developed into full-blooded ringing, had she not instantly lifted the receiver from its cradle and held it out towards Jack.

He took it gingerly and listened.

The voice he heard was strange. Perhaps deliberately disguised, and so crackly that he couldn't tell even whether it was male or female.

All the voice said was: "When the final one's been taken care of, the helicopter will be ready."

Then there was a click. And a dialling tone.

"So we can make contact with the outside world!" Maria whispered excitedly. "Are you going to call the police straight away?"

Jack shook his head. "Let's just check whether anyone tries to answer this first. It must have been a pre-arranged call at three o'clock. Change the wires back."

Maria did as he instructed. They left the office and hid in the alcove under the stairs to see if anyone came to the phone.

But no. Their presence must have frightened the enemy off. Though they dared not speak, both of them were thinking of the rustle they had heard as they approached the office, and in both minds the thought formed that that sound must have been made by the person for whom the mysterious call had been intended.

They waited till half-past three, but nothing stirred in Puzzel Manor.

Then Jack announced in a whisper that he was going to try to make a call.

"I'll come with you."

"No. Stay and keep guard. Give me the torch."

Maria saw the small beam settle on the office door-handle at the far side of the hall. It seemed to her that Jack opened the door rather noisily, but presumably he knew what he was doing. He closed it behind him, also rather noisily.

It wasn't more than a minute before he reappeared, hissing with frustration, "The line's dead. That one's been cut off now!"

"Ssh!" said Maria.

"Do you think it actually was 'The Executive Exterminator' on the phone?" she asked when they were back in the Yellow Room.

"No," said Jack Tarrant. "I've a feeling he's still around the Manor. No, that was just one of his acolytes. Some bent helicopter pilot, happy to take the money and not ask any questions."

Maria shivered. "What's horrible about the message is that it almost definitely means he intends another murder."

"I'm afraid, from the moment we knew we were up against 'The Executive Exterminator', there hasn't been any doubt of that."

"No." Maria cleared her throat and made her tone deliberately matter-of-fact. "I suppose we should prepare ourselves for the possibility that he'll go back to his old ways. In his choice of victim, I mean."

Jack's arms were suddenly round her waist, crushing her to him as if he would never let go. "I've been preparing myself for that possibility all along. Don't worry, love, I won't let you out of my sight."

"Of course," she said calmly, "I'm not the only one at risk."

"But you run your own company, you have beautiful hair, you –"

"Nerys."

Jack looked up at her in sudden alarm. But then a new thought struck him. He moved his watch up into the candlelight. "Five to four."

"What are you thinking?"

Jack's wheelchair was already speeding towards the door as he replied, "The last call on the fax line came at exactly three o'clock. It's quite possible that they've got an arrangement to ring every hour on the hour. We must go and see who comes!"

"But you said the line's down! And whoever was giving the message thinks he's already given it, anyway!"

Her words fell on emptiness. Jack Tarrant was already out of sight, speeding back towards the hall.

He was right. As they waited in the doorway, hardly breathing, their eyes straining against the darkness, they could just make out one of the residents of Puzzel Manor moving silently down the stairs, across the hall and into the office.

They looked at each other in wordless amazement.

Their quarry did not stay long and within a minute had retraced the route back upstairs.

They waited ten minutes, before Jack once again moved to the office. Maria followed him inside and closed the door.

She needed no telling to replace the fax plug with the phone plug again, and pick up the receiver.

"Dead. Like it was when you tried it."

"Hm. I wonder if it was five minutes ago . . . ?"

"You think they might be able to disconnect and reconnect it at will?"

"Not that difficult to do, if you can get at the wires."

"No. Of course, they could have done the same with the main phone line. And the electricity, come to that. It could all be part of a plot to isolate Puzzel Manor."

"Quite possible." Jack seemed abstracted.

"Well, maybe we can find out where they've disconnected it," Maria suggested enthusiastically.

"Maybe." He didn't sound that optimistic about the possibility.

"We must try! We must contact the police somehow."

"May not be possible." He pulled himself together. "At least Colonel Honeycutt's out there. He's our lifeline. He may well have reached the police by now."

"Hm. I wonder if there's some obvious clue here that we're missing . . . ?"

Maria's torchbeam moved restlessly across the room and stopped on a sheet of paper on the desk.

It was a *Times* crossword, apparently neatly cut out from a copy of the newspaper.

It certainly had not been in the office half an hour before.

She moved closer, looked down at the paper, and groaned.

"Bit of coat of arms on it?"

"Yes, Jack."

He wheeled his chair across and peered at the spotlit sheet. "Hm. Getting quite close to the bottom of the grid now."

"Getting close to the murderer revealing his name, perhaps?"

"Perhaps."

"Well, come on, Jack. You're the crossword expert. You spent all your time in hospital doing them."

"And when I came out, I swore I'd never look at another one."

"This one's important."

"You don't have to tell me."

"Get solving then."

"I don't think we have to solve the whole crossword."

"No?"

"No. I think one quarter of it should be enough."

"And what's the answer we're looking for – one word?"

"Yes. Or possibly just part of a word."

"Come on then, Jack – solve it!"

And he did.

BET YOU CAN'T DO THIS ONE, JACK! YOU HAVEN'T A CLUE!

ACROSS

1 Mistake - that rings a bell! (7)
5 Thinker journalist is hit over the head (7)
9 Aeroplane on one side in floral conflict (9)
10 One point not in, argues Guardian (5)
11 Eliot's name is heard as a vulgar Valhalla (5)
12 One of Israel's strays? (4,5)
14 Two donkeys, one states, for killings (14)
17 Done in a methodical way by computer programs (14)
21 East cooling east for a rocky time (9)
23 Ray Robinson's sweet (5)
24 Seizes a minced-up sirloin? (5)
25 Make a stab confusedly at the dodo? (2,2,5)
26 Sounds as if you have to soak the dwarf for a double picture (7)
27 Climbing apparatus runs on women's legs? (7)

DOWN

1 Blue or red could be said to be a selective killer (6)
2 Flowers put you in the record books (7)
3 Lass cages a setting for a museum exhibit (5,4)
4 Babies' toys upset a thespian Edmund for a reptile (11)
5 Watering-hole in the middle of backgammon (3)
6 A substantial command (5)
7 Toe-ring twisted for a Polynesian (7)
8 Princess of Wales's dark blue spread (8)
13 As slushy as Sterne's travels (11)
15 Oozed from dead turns? (15)
16 Like categorised - or mixed? (8)
18 Staff raised for a robbery (5-2)
19 An auditor and a pledge are all that are found in many cases (7)
20 I hear Archibald's found under the bridge (6)
25 This bit of music sounds as if it could make some bread (3)

To make
Elephant Pie
(to be taken with a Pinch
of Saltire!)

Take up four
Shoulders of
Sheep or two
of mixed
Admixture
Holstein Ale,
a River Plum
three Mullet
Patties,
Oxen - to
Elephant

1 DEAR	2 JACK TARRANT	3 THAT WAS THE	4 FIRST
5 MURDER	6 IT IS THE	7 TIME NEXT	8 FOR MURDER.
9 WHO WILL BE THE NEXT	10 VICTIM?	11 ANDERS ALTHIDSON	12 I AM
13 THE EXECUTIVE EXTERMINATOR	14 YOU DON'T KNOW	15	16 MY NAME IS.
17		18	
19			

HOW JACK AND MARIA
SOLVED THE TWELFTH PUZZLE:

The clue was in the word "saltire". Maria
recognised that it was a heraldic "ordinary" - a
diagonal cross, or "St Andrew's Cross", as featured
in the top right-hand quartering of the Puzzel coat of
arms. They imposed this shape on the recipe, and
were able to find the murderer's message, as shown
in the illustration.

FOURTEEN

BOXING DAY – 10.00 A.M.
COUNTRY WALK

T he latest tantalising piece of information – or misinforma-
tion or half-information – was slotted into its place on the
shield grid.

The possibilities it opened up were intriguing. The most
obvious – given the proximity between the words "MY NAME
IS" and the combination of letters from the crossword clue – was
intriguing in the extreme. Jack and Maria would have given
almost anything to know the letters that filled the gap between
those two answers.

They did not sleep at all that night, but spent the time planning.
After his brief collapse into defeatism, Jack Tarrant was now
more positive than ever. A plan was beginning to unfold in his
mind and during the small hours he went through it in every detail
with Maria, pulling it this way and that, feeling for flaws and
reworking it when they found any.

"I just hope to God it won't be necessary," he kept saying. "I
hope Colonel Honeycutt's got through and the police will be
arriving at any moment, but, just in case there is a hitch, I want to
be ready to put this plan into action."

So they worked on through the details, and by breakfast-time
had prepared themselves for every possible contingency.

They reckoned that, though Anders Altmidson was cunning
and vicious, they had stolen a march on him. Jack and Maria knew

151

who the accomplice was, and they felt pretty confident that "The Executive Exterminator" didn't know they knew.

The odds were now marginally better balanced than they had been before.

Most of the guests turned up for breakfast, and, after the slightly scratchy atmosphere of the evening before, all seemed more relaxed. The end of the Christmas Break was in sight, which was a relief, because the British are always hypersensitive to the danger of "having too much of a good thing".

Only Bob and Barbara Hood moaned (somewhat histrionically) about how they couldn't believe this really was the last day, and how they would miss all their new friends, and how awful it would be to go back to real life after all this "gracious living". (The fact that the snow looked set to keep them *in situ* for some days they did not mention.)

Roddy and Jan Stout, who apparently now had access to the locked kitchen and were helping Nerys to serve the breakfast, played cheerfully along with this banter. The proprietor did, however, keep looking at his watch. Jack and Maria felt confident that he was wondering how long the atmosphere of seasonal jollity could be sustained, before it was rudely shattered by the arrival of the police.

The only absentees from the guest list were, of course, the Honeycutts, and Trentham Metcalfe.

Peggy Smith-Brously came in late, her cheeks flushed from the cold air, telling everyone how lovely everything looked outside, and how, although the snow was very deep, it was possible to have "a little potter round". She liked to have a "constitutional" every day, she confided loudly to the assembly.

"Yes, well, it is important for the elderly to keep taking exercise, Mrs Brously-Smith," said Lady Deathridge, quite deliberately affronting her opponent both by the reference to her age and the misplacement of her precious hyphen.

Peggy Smith-Brously managed to curb her instinctive spit-back. "I do so agree," she said with a rigid smile. "Exercise does definitely increase one's life expectancy." She paused before the thrust. "I haven't noticed you taking much exercise, Lady Deathridge."

"Oh, don't worry. I've got a good few years left in me."

"I wouldn't be so sure of that," hissed Peggy Smith-Brously, on a spurt of venom which silenced the whole room.

Roddy Stout quickly came in to restore the equilibrium. His Christmas Break was probably already doomed by the approaching police; he didn't want animosity between his guests to hasten its collapse.

"Now, look, ladies and gentlemen . . ." He clapped his hands to signal what he hoped was a deft deflection of the conversation "You will all have seen from your brochures that what's supposed to be happening this morning is a 'Country Walk', followed by a 'Stirrup Cup with the Local Hunt'.

"Well, in spite of Mrs Smith-Brously's valiant pioneering efforts, I don't think the weather conditions really make walking an activity in which many of you are going to want – or even be able – to participate. And of course the Hunt is off, for obvious reasons.

"So I thought, instead, what we could do this morning is have a go at what we didn't get round to doing properly last night."

"What on earth are you drivelling about?" asked Celia Tranmere with gravelly truculence. She really did look very raddled that morning, as if she hadn't slept all night.

"I meant we could have a really good go at the 'Party Games'." The groan which greeted this suggestion was undisguised. "No, really. I mean, what was wrong last night was that *I* was running it and – though I say this against myself – I'm hopeless at that kind of thing."

"That is certainly true," Lady Deathridge concurred.

Trudy Bastable did not even look up. She was completely used to such gratuitous rudeness from her employer. Lady Deathridge's companion, Jack and Maria noted, looked tired, but otherwise apparently unscathed by her ordeal of the night before.

Roddy Stout decided to ignore the interruption. "What I'm saying is that this morning, with good old Trentham Metcalfe back in charge . . ." His eye travelled round the room, realising with increasing desperation that the actor was not present. "Well, I mean, I'm sure Trentham could get a jolly good atmosphere going, and you could all have a lot of fun and . . ."

He trailed away into unresponsive silence.

Count Leo Leontchy bailed the proprietor out with his customary studied politeness. "I think what you suggest, while of course a very attractive form of entertainment, is perhaps unnecessary. We are all here enjoying, I think, the comforts of Puzzel Manor. We are not children, we do not need every moment filled with diversions. We will be quite content to amuse ourselves this morning."

"Yes," Celia Tranmere agreed. "Let's ration out the thrills, for God's sake. It looks as if we could be here for some days, unless the weather breaks."

Lady Deathridge joined the conversation. "That is a point. How are we going to get away from here? It is imperative that I leave this afternoon. I have a dinner engagement in London."

"With this amount of snow," Roddy Stout apologised, "it really does look pretty unlikely that –"

"I would have thought it was part of the function of an hotelier," Lady Deathridge observed icily, "to ensure that his guests can travel to and from his premises."

"Under normal circumstances, of course, but –"

"Would you not regard it as normal to clear the snow from your driveways, so that vehicles may gain access?"

"Well, of course. When there's only a little snow, we –"

"Huh," Lady Deathridge pronounced contemptuously. "When the servant classes can't even make domestic arrangements work properly . . ."

Roddy Stout's face grew even more florid. Whatever his self-image may have been, it certainly wasn't as a member of "the servant classes". But he curbed his annoyance and crossed to the window. "There hasn't actually been any more snow overnight. I'm sure the ploughs have been out on the main roads, and it won't be long before they get through here," he continued with baseless optimism. "It doesn't look from those clouds as if there's likely to be any more snow."

The anxiety in his upward glance could have derived as easily from a fear of police helicopters as of snow.

He turned back to his guests with arms outspread in appeal.

"Anyway, is there really no one who would like to have a go at a few 'Party Games'? You know, 'Charades' . . . 'Clumps' . . . 'Are You There, Moriarty?' . . . ?"

But he got no takers. The only guest likely to have shown any enthusiasm for the suggestion, Alexander Honeycutt, was still presumably out with his father, trudging through the snow.

As Jack and Maria were leaving the dining room, they heard a clinking sound and arrived in the doorway of the Hunters' Bar just in time to see Trentham Metcalfe guiltily put something down behind the counter.

The Scotch was missing from the serried array of other upturned bottles, and it didn't take a genius to detect that the actor had just been having a quick slurp.

"Good morning," he said with a slight wince, as if each word bored into some particularly sensitive part of his brain.

"Good morning." The pleasantry dispensed with, Jack Tarrant moved straight on to the offensive. "You weren't in your bedroom last night."

The actor gaped at the suddenness of this attack. "Erm, well, no, I . . ."

"You were also seen creeping round the house in your Santa Claus get-up."

"What?" His amazement seemed genuine (but then, of course, he *was* an actor).

"All right, where were you last night?"

Maria Lethbury was content to let Jack conduct the interrogation, but she knew the psychological value of her presence. She watched the scene implacably, her arms folded across her chest.

"Well, I, er, well . . ." Trentham Metcalfe made an attempt at evasive charm. "Fact is, er . . . Do I have to tell you?"

"Yes."

"You see, I was brought up in a generation which exercised a little tact in these matters . . ."

"Where were you?"

"The fact is . . . erm, a lady is involved . . . and one doesn't

155

like to mention a lady's name in, er, this kind of context, erm . . ."

"Who was it?"

Trentham Metcalfe's defence collapsed quickly under this relentless bombardment. "Celia Tranmere," he confessed.

"Oh? And you spent the whole night together?"

"Yes. Well, I woke up last night about . . . what? Ten o'clock, I suppose – I'd had a little sleep in the evening – and then I went through to Celia's room."

"You had known each other before?"

"We'd worked together on a television play . . . fifteen years back, something like that. Location shooting in the Lake District, and we sort of palled up then."

"By 'palled up', do you mean that you became lovers?"

"Well, I think that's probably overstating it, but we certainly slept together a few times."

"Ah."

"Nothing serious. Were both married at the time, actually. But then that kind of thing always happens under those circs. You know," Trentham Metcalfe winked, "D.C.O.L."

"D.C.O.L.?"

"'Doesn't Count On Location.'"

"I see. So, last night . . . ?"

"Well, I woke up feeling a bit sort of . . . you know, randy – always been very highly sexed, as it happens – and I thought, why not pay a little visit to an old chum?"

"Celia?"

"Exactly." Another wink distorted the old actor's florid face. "Magic hadn't gone, let me tell you. All comes back. Like riding a bicycle, eh?"

Jack Tarrant had no interest in this kind of boasting, and moved quickly on. "So you did not at any time last evening go round the house dressed in the Santa Claus costume?"

"Good heavens, no. Took it off soon as I went upstairs after the Dickens reading." He referred to this with no apology. Perhaps his selective actor's memory had already translated it into one of his greatest performances. "What – did you think I went to bed with Celia wearing that lot? You imagine I'm some

156

kind of fetishist or something? Would have been totally in-
appropriate, anyway. Santa Claus is no good at all in that
department." He chuckled fruitily as he launched into another of
his jokes. "'Do you know why Santa Claus is such a lousy
lover?'"

"Trentham –"

But Jack was not quick enough to avert the punchline.
"'Because he only comes once a year and then he puts it in your
stocking!'"

Trentham Metcalfe found this inordinately funny. Nor did he
have the smile wiped off his face by Jack Tarrant's assertion that
his alibi would be checked out with the other party. He seemed to
have no anxiety that Celia Tranmere would not support his story.

She did confirm what he had said. Their accounts differed only in
one particular. In Celia's version of events, the "magic" certainly
had gone, and if Trentham Metcalfe's bicycling skills matched his
love-making, then he'd have forgotten even how to get on the
saddle.

Apparently, after one failed attempt at intimacy, he had lain
half-across her all night, snoring like a walrus and asphyxiating
her with stale whisky.

They were crossing the hall after their encounter with Celia,
when Maria chanced to look out through the window on which,
what seemed like a year before, the Rev. Verdure had tapped at
the end of Trentham Metcalfe's Ghost Story.

"Look!"

Jack's eyes followed her pointing finger to a small, exhausted
figure tramping across the snow towards the house.

"It's Alexander Honeycutt!"

Roddy Stout was alerted, and he and Bob Hood quickly donned
gumboots and went to help the boy in. He looked wrecked, his
young face pinched and pale. His frozen garments were removed
and he was sat down in front of the hall fire, wrapped in blankets,
while Jan Stout hurried off to heat up some soup for him.

The guests gathered round, as Jack Tarrant asked the boy,
very gently, what had happened. "And where's your father?"

Alexander Honeycutt was breathing heavily as he replied, "He fell. In a drift. He was hurt."

"How badly hurt?"

There was the minutest hesitation before the boy answered, "He broke his leg."

"Where did it happen?"

"I don't know. Maybe a mile away. It's hard to tell in the snow."

"How long did it take you to get back from there?"

Alexander Honeycutt looked at his watch. "Two hours? Three hours?"

"God, the poor man's been lying in the cold all that time."

"Just think of the risk of hypothermia," said Barbara Hood.

"He'll be OK. He's a very fit man," her husband asserted, nodding his head towards the boy.

Barbara got the message. "Oh yes, sure. He'll be fine. No problem."

"Somebody'd better go out and find him," said Jack. "It shouldn't be difficult – you just follow Alexander's tracks."

"But be very careful," the boy advised. "It really is dreadful out there."

"There's a sledge in the coach-house," Roddy Stout remembered. "We'd better take that to bring him back on."

"The snow may be too deep for a sledge," said Alexander. "You may have to carry him."

"Yes. Well, in that case, the search party had better be all the men," Bob Hood suggested.

"Except for me, I'm afraid." Jack Tarrant gestured impotently at his wheelchair.

"Except for you, of course."

And so it was agreed. Count Leo Leontchy, Trentham Metcalfe and Bob Hood all went off to their rooms to wrap themselves in layers of warm garments. Roddy Stout did the same, but his clothes were there in the hall. As he put them on, he casually asked Alexander Honeycutt, "So your father was injured before you managed to make contact with the police?"

"Oh yes. We still couldn't even see the village."

"Dear oh dear. What a pity."

But even as he said the words, triumph and relief gleamed in Roddy Stout's eyes. It looked as if his Christmas Break would not be disrupted, after all.

Alexander's news also had implications for Jack Tarrant. But for him they were much darker.

The police were not coming. There would be no one to assist him and Maria in their battle with "The Executive Exterminator".

After the search party had left, the boy lay drowsily sipping the soup that Jan Stout had brought him.

"You hesitated," Jack Tarrant said softly, "when you told us that your father had broken his leg . . ."

"Yes." Alexander Honeycutt looked alarmed and a little guilty. "Yes, I did."

"And was it true?"

"Well . . . Well, it's what my father said I should say."

"You mean, you don't think he had broken his leg?"

"If he had, it caused a lot of blood."

"Blood?"

"Yes. All over the snow."

"Tell me exactly what happened."

"Well, my father's bigger than me, and stronger – obviously he is – and he kept getting further ahead, and I kept hurrying to catch up, and then he'd wait for me, and get very cross because I was being so slow."

"He didn't strike me as a particularly patient man."

"That, Mr Tarrant, is an understatement. My father's temper is . . . well, never mind. Anyway, he'd got quite a long way ahead, and I just followed his footprints, and then I found him . . . and his trouser leg was soaked in blood, and there was blood on the snow all around."

"That's pretty unlikely for a broken leg – if he'd just done it in the snow."

"Yes. Actually, it didn't look at all as if he'd broken his leg."

"What did it look like, Alexander?"

"It looked as if he'd been shot."

A few minutes after this, the boy yawned.

"I think it's time I took you up to bed, young man," said Maria.

"Yes. I am pretty tired, actually."

"Hardly surprising. I'll tuck you up."

"I say, Miss Lethbury . . ."

"Yes?"

"You wouldn't play a game with me upstairs, would you? Just till I go to sleep?"

"Course I will. What sort of game?"

"Oh, one of these."

Alexander Honeycutt reached forward to the pile of boardgames on a fireside table. Monopoly. Scrabble. Cluedo.

"What's that one?" Maria pointed to a faded blue box, on which the words "DOUBLE DIBBLE" were picked out in tarnished gold.

"Oh, that's most peculiar. Very old, I think. I tried reading the rules, but I couldn't make head or tail of them."

"So which one do you want to play, Alexander?"

"Cluedo?"

"All right." Maria grinned. "I'm just going upstairs, Jack, and, er . . . may be some time."

"All right," said Jack absent-mindedly, as he reached forward to pick up the "DOUBLE DIBBLE" box.

Alexander Honeycutt yawned hugely as he stood up. Then something outside the window caught his attention. "I say, someone's been playing with my snowman."

"Oh?"

"Look, it's a lot taller than how I made it."

Jack Tarrant looked curiously out of the window. "Yes. Yes, it is, isn't it?"

Alexander yawned again.

"Come on, up you come," said Maria.

"Yes. Up we go, Miss Lethbury."

"See you, Jack."

"See you, Maria," said Jack, apparently forgetting his vow not to let her out of his sight.

*

By the end of their game, Alexander Honeycutt was nearly asleep. "We play Cluedo quite a lot at school," he confided drowsily. "In the dorm."

"Do you like school?"

There was no questioning the genuine enthusiasm in his reply, "Yes, it's terrific."

"And the rest of the time you spend mostly with your aunt?"

"Yes. She's Mummy – my mother's sister," he hastily corrected himself. Thirteen-year-olds at public school feel they're showing themselves up by saying "Mummy".

"And you get on with her?"

"Oh, she's lovely. She's . . . well, it's almost like having Mu – my mother back."

"And how do you get on with your father?"

"Well . . ." Sleepiness weakened the boy's loyalty. "He's not the easiest personality in the world . . ."

"No. I'm sure he isn't . . ."

Seconds later, the boy was asleep.

Maria Lethbury watched him for a few minutes, but then heard a footstep passing on the landing. She silently left the bedroom to investigate.

Using one hand to wheel himself along to the Yellow Room, with the other Jack Tarrant opened the box of "DOUBLE DIBBLE".

As Alexander Honeycutt had said, it appeared to be a very old game. And a most peculiar one. There was a strange, irregularly striped board, a selection of bizarrely shaped wooden pieces, and a set of rules printed on greying paper.

Jack needed both hands to manoeuvre the wheelchair into the Yellow Room, so he put the game's rules back without looking at them. And once inside, he moved immediately to the window.

With some difficulty, he managed to raise the sash, and looked out at Alexander Honeycutt's snowman. The boy had been right. There was no doubt the structure was a good foot taller than it had been the day before.

Jack pressed together snow from the sill into a firm hard missile, took careful aim, and hurled it out of the window.

The first snowball missed, but the second landed full on the snowman's face.

The surface cracked and a little plate of snow slipped down. Underneath was something that didn't look at all like snow.

Trembling with anticipation, Jack crammed together another snowball, and threw it.

The front of the snowman's head crumbled away, and Jack Tarrant found himself looking into the frozen, dead face of Anders Altmidson.

It had all been a double bluff. The murder in the kitchen had been for real.

And, if the chef was really dead, that had to mean that someone else was "The Executive Exterminator".

Someone else who was possibly, even at that moment, stalking round Puzzel Manor.

Pausing only to close the window, Jack swung the wheels of his chair round and started for the door.

But, out of the corner of his eye, he saw the open box of "DOUBLE DIBBLE", with the rules lying on top.

And in the upper right-hand corner of those rules, he saw a symbol he recognised.

He picked up the paper and looked at it.

"I see," thought Jack Tarrant feverishly. "Just looking for one word here. And no doubt I'll find it, by a process of trial and error . . ."

THE OLD ENGLISH GAME OF "DOUBLE DIBBLE" (OR "MOSES AND AARON")

The history of the game is said to go back to the Saxon era, and there is even a rumour that it was played by King Canute before his confrontation with the sea. It is certainly very ancient, and yet retains today just as much appeal as it always had.

DOUBLE DIBBLE is played on a board marked with irregular striations, which become closer together towards the outer edges (or "yards"). The traditional game is played by two players, each of whom has command of seven small counters (or "plugs") and twwo larger counters, one round (the "Moses") and one square (the "Aaron"). The Northumberland version of the game, in which each player also has a triangular counter (the "Pentecost"), need not concern us here.

THE AIM OF THE GAME

Each player aims to "compromise" both his opponent's "Moses" and "Aaron" in their own "yard", without sacrificing more than three of his own "plugs". A full victory is called a "trouser-button". A victory in whhich more than three "plugs" are forfeited is called "a melted ice". In scoring over a sequence of games, three "melted ices" have the same value as two "trouser-buttons". Each "trouser-button" counts for two points (or "thimbles"), and the winner (or "cream-bearer") of a full game of DOUBLE-DIBBLE is the first player to reach a score of twelve "thimbles" (a "bolster").

STARTING TO PLAY

Each player begins by setting out four "plugs" on any of the first five striations in his "yard". No more than two "plugs" may be placed on any one striation, except for the widest (the "yard gallery"), on which three may be placed. Each player then rolls the hexagonal wooden dice (or "cheese"), and the first one to roll a "pigeon" (marked on the "cheese" by a double cross) can choose whether to put out his "Moses" or his "Aaaron" on the corner square of his "yard" (known as the "keepsake"). The player who did not roll a "pigeon" is then obliged to put out the other counter (his "Moses" if his opponent has put out an "Aaron", and vice-versa). Because of the different moves available to the two counters, the advantage of this initial choice is obviously considerable.

THE BASIC MOVES

At the risk of oversimplification, it can be stated that "plugs" can only move on the transverse opposing diagonal; the "Moses" can move three striations forwards and two backwards in any combination, except when that move takes the counter on to a striation already occupied by either the player's own or his opponent's "Aaron"; and the "Aaron" can move two striations forwards and three backwards in any combination, except when that move takes him on to a striation adjacent to one already occupied by one of his own "plugs". Moves are taken in turn, according to the roll of the "cheese". A "pigeon" (two crosses), a "mallard" (one cross) or a "gannet" (one diagonal slash) all count for a move of one striation; while a "beef" (two diagonal slashes), a "muttton" (one ring) or a "pork" (two interlinked rings) count for a move of three striations (except when the opposing player's "Aaron" is in "umbrage", which

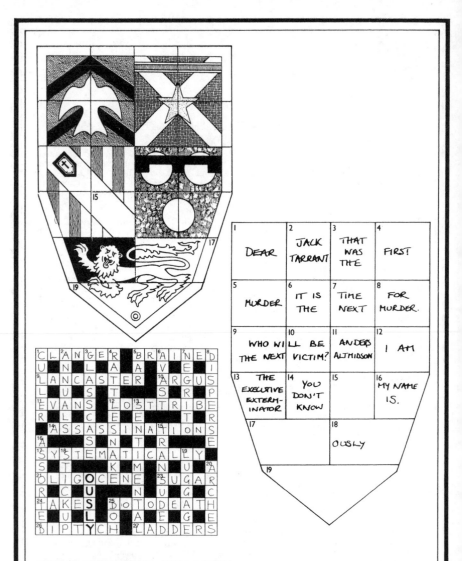

The crossword grid contains the answers: CLANGER, BRAINED, LANCASTER, ARGUS, EVANS, LOSTTRIBE, ASSASSINATIONS, SYSTEMATICALLY, OLIGOCENE, SUGAR, RAKES, DOTODEATH, DIPTYCH, LADDERS.

The message grid:

1 DEAR	2 JACK TARRANT	3 THAT WAS THE	4 FIRST
5 MURDER	6 IT IS THE	7 TIME NEXT	8 FOR MURDER.
9 WHO WILL BE THE NEXT	10 VICTIM?	11 ANDERS ALTHIDSON	12 I AM
13 THE EXECUTIVE EXTERMINATOR	14 YOU DON'T KNOW	15	16 MY NAME IS.
17		18 OUSLY	
19			

THIS IS HOW JACK AND MARIA SOLVED THE THIRTEENTH PUZZLE:

They quickly realised that they didn't have to complete the whole crossword (though the solution is given above for anyone who actually did take that trouble!), but that the answer they were looking for would fit into the unnumbered space, which should have been "22 Down". Clues were given to this by the fact that the Crossword Puzzle was numbered "22", by the murderer's hint ("You haven't a clue!"), and by the "U" and the "L" already filled in.

FIFTEEN

BOXING DAY – 12.30 P.M.
LOCAL HUNT

"I've looked," said Nerys, as she came down the stairs. "Maria's not up there."

"Oh." Jack Tarrant's voice had the timbre of someone trying a little too hard to sound unconcerned. "Alexander is, though?"

"In bed, yes. Out cold, poor little mite. Hardly surprising, after what he went through last night. There's a game of Cluedo spread out on the bedside table – Miss Scarlett Did It in the Conservatory with the Lead Piping, if you happen to be interested – but there's no sign of Maria, I'm afraid."

Jack said lightly, "Oh well. Never mind."

Nerys moved on across the hall. "If I see her, I'll say you were looking for her."

"Thank you."

As the girl went in through the office door, Jack Tarrant was once again aware of her trim body in its neat dark suit, and her heavy, swaying black hair. A new *frisson* of fear ran through him.

Swiftly, but without any appearance of panic, he wheeled himself across to the kitchen door. It was no longer locked, and he pushed it open.

"Excuse me, Mrs Stout. Have you by any chance seen Maria?"

Jan Stout looked up from chopping lettuce. Perhaps she did not know that the scrubbed pine table on which she was working had recently been graced by her chef's corpse. Perhaps she did not even know that Anders Altmidson had disappeared. Either way, she seemed supremely unconcerned.

"No, I haven't. Didn't she go upstairs to put young Alexander Honeycutt to bed?"

"Yes, she did."

"Well, she's probably still up there with him then."

"Yes. Yes, probably."

The other female guests were in the south drawing room. Celia Tranmere had a magazine open on her lap, but the sleepless night had caught up with her. Her eyes were closed and her mouth slackly open, emitting an unladylike rasping sound.

Barbara Hood and Peggy Smith-Brously were both reading magazines, while Lady Deathridge had found a Debrett's *Peerage*, which she was scrutinising with considerable relish. At a small table by herself, Trudy Bastable was playing out a complicated game of Patience.

"Oh, hello," said Jack, as his wheelchair appeared in the doorway. "I wondered if any of you had seen Maria. My girlfriend, Maria Lethbury."

Celia Tranmere did not wake, but the others shook their heads apologetically.

"Well, at least, in our current circumstances," observed Lady Deathridge, "you can be pretty certain she hasn't walked out on you. It would be virtually impossible – even if she wanted to."

Peggy Smith-Brously gave him a condescending smile. "It must be very inconvenient for you, being without your girlfriend. Really does restrict your movements, having no one to push you about, doesn't it?"

Someone hypersensitive might have detected a note of triumph in her words. Or maybe it was just the customary arrogance of the Smith-Brously manner.

"I'll push you, if you want to go anywhere."

These unexpected words were quietly spoken. Trudy Bastable rose from her Patience, picked up her handbag, and moved towards the door.

"That is, if there's nothing you require me for at the moment, Lady Deathridge . . . ?"

Her employer waved a curt permission to leave. Trudy moved behind Jack's wheelchair, slinging the strap of her handbag over her shoulder. She took the handles with practised ease, swivelled the chair round and pushed it into the middle of the hall.

"Anywhere you particularly want to go, Mr Tarrant?"

"Do you know where the ice-house is?"

"No."

"It's in the back yard."

Jan Stout was no longer in the kitchen, as Trudy pushed him through.

"Could you pick up that torch on the dresser?"

She handed it to him, then skilfully negotiated the back step and directed the wheelchair straight to the ice-house door. Jack was already reaching into his pocket for the picklock, but the padlock hung open on its ring.

"You want to go inside?" asked Trudy Bastable.

Jack Tarrant nodded, as if too overcome for words.

She reached forward and pulled back the doors, one by one. Jack shone the torch down the steps, but the low lintel of the doorway cut off the room's recesses from his sight.

He felt Trudy Bastable's strong hands grasp the handles of the wheelchair, which she manoeuvred efficiently down the steps into the ice-house.

Reluctantly, he swung the beam of his torch across the stacked furniture at the back. The cot, together with its murdered contents, had disappeared.

But, against the furthest wall, there was a new horror.

It was as in his dream. Maria Lethbury's body sagged from a plastic-covered cord attached to a large hook in the ceiling. She was dressed in a dark suit, very like the one Nerys had been wearing the day before.

On the precious, unmoving face the garish parody of make-up gleamed mockingly.

And her hair, her glorious red hair, had all gone, leaving only a haze of blue stubble on a head which now looked shrunken and defenceless, like a baby's.

167

"Oh, no!" The words were hardly distinguishable in the great groan which shuddered through Jack Tarrant's body. "Too late! I was too late!"

He wheeled himself forward and, as in his nightmare, reached up to touch one shoeless, stockinged foot.

"Still warm," he moaned. "Only a few minutes too late!"

Taking a grip of the foot, he eased the body round and focused his torchbeam on the back of its jacket.

"There's nothing there. No message."

He heard a rustling on the floor behind him.

"Is this what you're looking for? It must have dropped down."

Trudy Bastable handed him a sheet of paper.

It was, as expected, a "With Compliments" slip.

And on it were two segments of the Puzzel coat of arms.

Jack Tarrant's body trembled as he looked at the puzzle. "It's an easy one," he said despairingly. "As if it mattered. As if anything mattered now. I'm too late!" he sobbed. "Too late!

"There's no question about it now – he's won. 'The Executive Exterminator' has taken the only thing I've ever truly cared about! He's beaten Jack Tarrant!"

THE OLD ENGLISH GAME OF "DOUBLE DIBBLE" (OR "MOSES AND AARON")

The history of the game is said to go back to the Saxon era, and there is even a rumour that it was played by King Canute before his confrontation with the sea. It is certainly very ancient, and yet retains today just as much appeal as it always had.

DOUBLE DIBBLE is played on a board marked with irregular striations, which become closer together towards the outer edges (or "yards"). The traditional game is played by two players, each of whom has command of seven small counters (or "plugs") and twwo **W** larger counters, one round (the "Moses") and one square (the "Aaron"). The Northumberland version of the game, in which each player also has a triangular counter (the "Pentecost"), need not concern us here.

THE AIM OF THE GAME

Each player aims to "compromise" both his opponent's "Moses" and "Aaron" in their own "yard", without sacrificing more than three of his own "plugs". A full victory is called a "trouser-button". A victory in whhich more than three "plugs" are forfeited is called "a **H** melted ice". In scoring over a sequence of games, three "melted ices" have the same value as two "trouser-buttons". Each "trouser-button" counts for two points (or "thimbles"), and the winner (or "cream-bearer") of a full game of DOUBLE-DIBBLE is the first player to reach a score of twelve "thimbles" (a "bolster").

STARTING TO PLAY

Each player begins by setting out four "plugs" on any of the first five striations in his "yard". No more than two "plugs" may be placed on any one striation, except for the widest (the "yard gallery"), on which three may be placed. Each player then rolls the hexagonal wooden dice (or "cheese"), and the first one to roll a "pigeon" (marked on the "cheese" by a double cross) can choose whether to put out his "Moses" or his "Aaaron" on the corner square **A** of his "yard" (known as the "keepsake"). The player who did not roll a "pigeon" is then obliged to put out the other counter (his "Moses" if his opponent has put out an "Aaron", and vice-versa). Because of the different moves available to the two counters, the advantage of this initial choice is obviously considerable.

THE BASIC MOVES

At the risk of oversimplification, it can be stated that "plugs" can only move on the transverse opposing diagonal; the "Moses" can move three striations forwards and two backwards in any combination, except when that move takes the counter on to a striation already occupied by either the player's own or his opponent's "Aaron"; and the "Aaron" can move two striations forwards and three backwards in any combination, except when that move takes him on to a striation adjacent to one already occupied by one of his own "plugs". Moves are taken in turn, according to the roll of the "cheese". A "pigeon" (two crosses), a "mallard" (one cross) or a "gannet" (one diagonal slash) all count for a move of one striation; while a "beef" (two diagonal slashes), a "muttton" (one ring) or a **T** "pork" (two interlinked rings) count for a move of three striations (except when the opposing player's "Aaron" is in "umbrage", which

THIS IS HOW JACK
SOLVED THE FOURTEENTH PUZZLE:
Recognising that the puzzle's secret was typographical, Jack looked for extra letters in the text, and found the solution as demonstrated above.

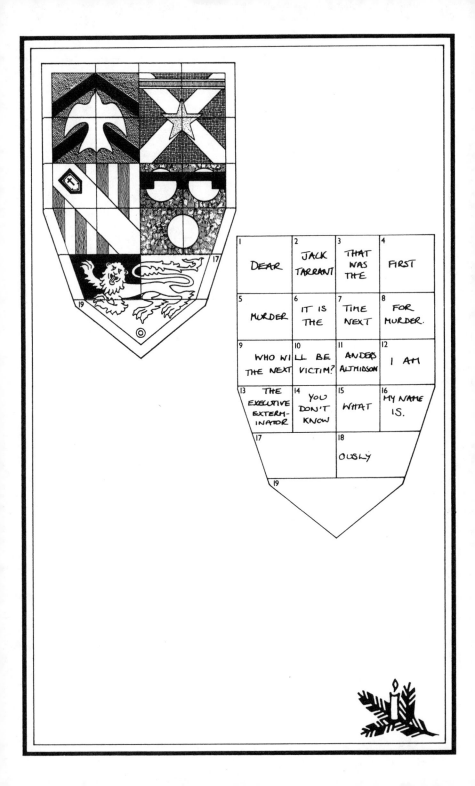

1 DEAR	2 JACK TARRANT	3 THAT WAS THE	4 FIRST
5 MURDER	6 IT IS THE	7 TIME NEXT	8 FOR MURDER.
9 WHO WILL BE THE NEXT	10 LL BE VICTIM?	11 ANDERS ALTHIDSON	12 I AM
13 THE EXECUTIVE EXTERMINATOR	14 YOU DON'T KNOW	15 WHAT	16 MY NAME IS.
17	18 OUSLY		
19			

SIXTEEN

BOXING DAY – AFTERNOON. DEPARTURE

She sat opposite him in the Yellow Room. An evil smile played around her lips, and the likeness was so marked Jack couldn't imagine why he hadn't noticed it before.

"You're his sister, aren't you?"

Trudy Bastable – or whatever her real name was – nodded.

"And he did it for you. You were the reason for the killings – all of them."

"Yes. We were a very close family," she said in a poisonous whisper. "He and I were particularly close. All through our childhood we never played with other children. It was always just him and me, playing endless games, games of which we never tired."

"Games and puzzles . . ."

"Exactly. Games and puzzles and mock-murders. He was always very good at setting up little scenes with lots of false blood all over the place."

"Just as he did to make Anders Altmidson's death look like a set-up?"

She nodded jubilantly. "Yes, we always loved tricks like that."

"And – of course! – it was your scream that distracted me from taking a proper look at Anders' body. You never saw anyone in a Santa Claus suit, did you?"

Triumphantly, she shook her head.

Jack shook his too, but not in triumph. "I should have realised then."

"Yes, you should, but you didn't. Mind you, you did pretty well with the puzzles," she conceded.

"Thank you."

She smiled at some distant recollection. "Of course, I was always better at devising and doing puzzles than my brother was. His mind never worked quite as deviously as mine."

"Was he jealous of your skills?"

"Oh no. His admiration for me has always been unlimited." Her face darkened. "He could never understand why the rest of the world didn't appreciate me as much as he did."

"Which was why he decided that the rest of the world should be taught a lesson?"

"Why *I* decided that, yes," she replied coyly.

"So you're the one who's been responsible for all the fiendish puzzles here at Puzzel Manor, are you?"

"Yes. Every one of them. And, by the way, thank you. I take the word 'fiendish' as a compliment."

"You were the brains behind the whole thing? Your brother was never more than your hitman?"

"He was a bit more than that . . . but yes, I was the one who planned everything. And he carried it all out for me. He's always done exactly what I've wanted. Very powerful emotion, you know, brotherly love."

"Particularly between you two."

"Yes. And, to forestall your next, undoubtedly prurient, question, I do mean love in the fullest sense. He and I have been lovers since we were in our teens. That's why we set up different identities for ourselves, even why he got married. To avert suspicion. The world has always had a ridiculously old-fashioned attitude to true family love." She smiled winsomely. "No, he's always been very protective towards me."

"I would say what he's done for you deserves a stronger word than 'protective'."

She laughed. It was not an attractive sound. "He could never bear to see me hurt, you see. But the world can be a hurtful place – particularly hurtful for a woman who is not, by that world's standards, attractive . . ." The bitterness in her voice grew stronger – ". . . a woman who doesn't have a good figure, who doesn't have beautiful hair. The world is designed for the beautiful people, not for people like me."

"That's why those were the ones you targeted? So it meant that, with you and your brother at large, any beautiful woman with beautiful hair was at risk . . ."

"Not *any* woman," she rebuked him sharply. "You make it sound as if our killings were random, indiscriminate. Oh no, we chose who was going to die with great care. For a start, it had to be a woman with power."

"An executive."

She nodded. "Neither of us approved of aggressive career women. We thought women should be properly subservient to men."

"I wouldn't have thought the way you dominate your brother is a very good example of subservience."

"It's all a matter of how things are done!" she snapped, and then recovered herself. "In company, I am always quiet and demure, as a woman should be."

"And you don't think women should have jobs?"

"I didn't say that. I don't think women should behave in their jobs as men do. But I certainly think women should work. We've got lots of family money and I still work. I've worked all my adult life, but I've always been ladylike about it."

"What, acting as companion to Lady Deathridge?"

"No. That's very recent. Just a means to an end. I'd discovered she had booked in here months ago. She's such a poisonous old bat that none of her companions last very long, so I just had to wait for her next advertisement to appear in the *Lady* and then apply."

"Why?"

"So that I could be here at Puzzel Manor to set up all the *games*."

If nothing else had done it, the glee which she put into the word "games" showed that she was without doubt certifiably insane.

"So this whole charade was set up to get at me?"

"Yes, Jack Tarrant. Of course it was. You should be flattered. You see, you got too close to catching 'The Executive Exterminator'. My brother and I didn't like that. We decided that you needed to be taught a lesson."

He grimaced. "You didn't think the bullet in my hip which confined me to this bloody wheelchair was enough lesson?"

She smiled sweetly. "Oh no. Not nearly enough."

Jack sighed, and redirected the conversation. "So what did you do before you were taken on by Lady Deathridge?"

"I worked for a sandwich company in the City. My job was delivering sandwiches to the offices that had ordered them. And some of the people I delivered them to were very polite . . . and some behaved as if I didn't exist . . ."

"You're talking about women now?"

"Of course. It's all right for a man not to notice someone who comes into his office with a box of sandwiches. That's a man's prerogative."

"But not a woman's?"

She shook her head smugly. "Oh no. Certainly not."

"So that was it? That was the link between the murder victims? Any attractive woman executive who didn't say 'thank you' when you delivered her sandwiches had just signed her own death warrant?"

"Pretty well, yes." She smiled girlishly. "Neat, wasn't it? I'm surprised the police never made the connection."

"No, it was stupid of us."

"Ah, but you see, there are advantages to being the kind of person nobody notices. I must have walked in and out of twenty offices a day, and I'm sure, if questioned afterwards, almost no one working in them would have remembered me."

"No. So, how did you decide to commit the first murder?"

"I'll tell you." She reached into her handbag and pulled out a walkie-talkie transmitter, which she placed on the low table in front of her.

"I'll be getting a call from my brother in the helicopter soon. And then I'm afraid I'll have to leave you – leave you alone with your failure, Jack Tarrant. But, until the call comes, I'm more than happy to tell you all about our murders."

And she told him. Everything. Every single step of the meticulous planning that preceded each killing, every detail of the siblings' lunatic rituals of homicide.

"And Vanessa Dickinson?" Jack interjected at one point. "She was Alexander Honeycutt's mother, wasn't she?"

"Oh yes," said Trudy Bastable with great satisfaction. "Yes, she was."

At the end of the gruesome catalogue, Jack said, "But the murders here . . . they were different, weren't they?"

Her unnerving little smile returned. "Very different. My brother and I didn't want to repeat ourselves, didn't want to get stale, you see. No, we thought we'd set up something . . . more exciting for here."

"But you must have known all about the Puzzel family history, the hereditary missing toe, the effect of the snow on Gervaise –"

This sent her off into peals of girlish laughter. "Oh, we *did* catch you out so beautifully, didn't we, Jack Tarrant? I made all that up. It was absolute nonsense."

"So the first murder victim wasn't related to the Puzzels?"

"No. When we started doing our research, we discovered that Celia Tranmere's lover, Anton Brown, had one toe missing. That was my springboard – that's what inspired me to invent all those wonderful stories," she concluded with ladylike pride.

"So all that business about the Puzzel family history . . . everything in the Ghost Story – you made it all up?"

She nodded, hugging herself for her cleverness.

"But how did you persuade Trentham Metcalfe to read the Ghost Story?"

"No persuasion needed. The Stouts hadn't really made any preparations for that side of the programme. They assumed Trentham would find some suitable stuff and – needless to say, given the kind of shambolic character he is – he hadn't brought anything with him. So I just left my story lying around where he was bound to come across it. I knew there was no way an old ham like him could resist its dramatic possibilities."

"I see. So there was no logic at all to the murders. They were

177

just set up to lead me a merry dance."

"Precisely," she said, with that insouciance for the value of human life that marks out the psychopath.

"But . . ." Jack groaned as he spoke the name – "why Maria? She'd never been rude or dismissive to you."

"No. We had to kill Maria Lethbury to show how completely we were in charge. To show that my brother and I have defeated you, Jack Tarrant, totally and utterly. And, what's more, that we'll never be caught."

"No." In his wheelchair Jack Tarrant looked suddenly old and shrunken with despair.

"From the moment my brother left the house, I knew it was only a matter of time before Maria Lethbury's body would be found. I thought he'd let me know where it was, so that I could attach the 'With Compliments' puzzle, but clearly he didn't get the chance. It didn't matter, though. It all worked perfectly.

"And that was the signal we'd agreed. As soon as you saw Maria Lethbury's body, we knew you'd be finished, Jack Tarrant. And we knew that we would successfully have completed all the Christmas Crimes at Puzzel Manor."

He was incapable of reply.

At that moment "Trudy Bastable"'s walkie-talkie crackled into life. "Yes?" she said, lifting it to her ear.

The voice was male, but heard through so much electrical interference that one could not have identified it more precisely. *"Calling Trudy Bastable. Helicopter approaching Puzzel Manor. Will hover over front lawn and lower cradle for you."*

"I'll be ready for it," she said, and triumphantly switched off the receiver. She looked at her watch. "Perfect timing. The Departure, like everything else for the past two days, has gone exactly to plan."

She moved to the window, and easily raised the sash, letting in the hum of the approaching helicopter. Then she turned back gleefully to her victim. "I'll leave you the walkie-talkie. I'm sure my brother would love to have a quick word with you, Jack Tarrant . . . before we vanish out of your life for ever."

Jack, with the appearance of a totally broken man, said nothing.

"Trudy Bastable" again looked out of the window. The helicopter hum was louder than ever. "Going to have to leave you now, I'm afraid, Jack Tarrant."

She straddled the window-sill and lowered herself on to the snow with surprising agility. She looked at the snowman, from which the dead, frozen face of Anders Altmidson stared bleakly out, and allowed herself a little smile.

"You know, I really do think that was one of our best touches, don't you?"

There was no reply.

With a peal of the laughter that already haunted Jack Tarrant, and would now haunt him for the rest of his life, "Trudy Bastable" hurried nimbly across the snow towards the cradle that had appeared, dangling down from the hovering helicopter.

She sat neatly in it and, with a mocking wave towards her defeated adversary, started to rise up into the air.

Jack Tarrant slumped unmoving in his posture of defeat.

Then the walkie-talkie on the table crackled once again.

Shaking his head to dislodge the accumulation of thoughts inside it, he reached forward to pick up the instrument.

"Yes?"

"Is that Jack Tarrant?"

"Speaking."

"She's safely in the helicopter."

"Any problems?"

"She put up a fight, but we overpowered her."

"And the brother?"

"Picked him up without too much difficulty. He wasn't far away from the house."

"Good."

"And did you get the confession you wanted?"

"Oh yes." Jack Tarrant produced a small cassette recorder from his jacket pocket and placed it on the table. "Chapter and verse of every single murder. There's enough here to put them both in a secure institution for any number of life sentences."

"Well done." There was an awkward static-filled pause. *"That*

*must be some compensation for you, Jack – you know, for every-
thing you've suffered."*

"For everything I've suffered," Jack Tarrant echoed dully.
"Thanks for all you've done. We'll talk soon."

He let the walkie-talkie drop from his fingers on to the table,
and slowly turned his wheelchair to face the window. He looked
out towards the main gates of Puzzel Manor.

The thaw had begun. From the tip of the murdered Anders
Altmidson's nose, a drop of liquid hung obscenely. Some of the
snow had slipped from the yew tree down by the entrance to the
Puzzel Manor grounds and the dark green of the leaves showed
through.

A long melancholy sigh escaped from Jack Tarrant's lips. The
residents of Puzzel Manor were now safe. Their danger was
past.

But at what cost?

So preoccupied was he that he did not hear the door of the
Yellow Room open behind him. Nor did he hear the soft footsteps
of the cowled figure in the Santa Claus costume moving towards
him with hands outstretched.

It was only when they touched his neck that his own hands
leapt up to grasp them. They struggled for a moment, and in the
confusion the Santa Claus hood slipped off.

"Hello, Baldie," said Jack.

"It'll grow again," said Maria, slipping off her white beard. She
had removed the hideous make-up, and her face, without its
frame of hair, looked elf-like.

She closed the window and came round to sit on Jack's lap in
the safe cradle of his arms. "But was it worth it?"

"Oh yes. It was worth it. I've just heard from the helicopter.
They've got both of them. And . . ." he indicated the cassette
recorder – "I've got the most detailed confession any court in the
world could ever ask for."

"I was so scared when she came into the ice-house with you, I
thought I was going to spoil it all by trembling."

"You did beautifully."

"Really uncomfortable in that harness, though. It felt as if it
was sawing through my armpits."

180

"Time enough to recover, Maria. We've got all the time in the world now. And it *was* worth it, it really was."

"I know. I thought she was going to be suspicious because I hadn't got the 'With Compliments' slip stapled on that jacket of Nerys's."

"No, that was all right, because, you see, *she* did all the puzzles and *he* did all the murders. She had expected he'd let her know where your body was, but assumed that I just found you before he'd had a chance to do so. So she didn't find the 'With Compliments' slip on the floor. She just got it out of her handbag."

"Right." A shudder ran through Maria's body. "Thank God it's over. The police played their part beautifully."

"Yes. I still seem to have a bit of influence, even though I'm pensioned off."

"You spoke to them early this morning when you went back into the office to try the fax line, didn't you?"

"That was it. It was still connected then. I didn't have long, but I managed to persuade them. I told them it was worth the risk of another murder to ensure that we got the confession. In fact, I took complete responsibility for that risk."

"And that was why you made so much noise going into the office and coming out?"

"Yes. I knew Trudy was listening – well, at that stage we didn't know it was Trudy . . ."

"Didn't know that till we saw her going into the office later."

"No, but I knew there was someone listening, and I wanted them to think that I thought the fax line was broken."

"Yes. And thank God it all worked."

Suddenly they heard the unexpected sound of the telephone ringing.

"Good Lord, must have been reconnected." Maria got up out of Jack's lap and went across to answer it.

"Yes. Yes, fine. See you then." She put the receiver down. "Police helicopter will be coming back for us in about half an hour."

"Great," said Jack. "And then what shall we do, Maria?"

"Well, I think, after all this, we could use a break."

"You can say that again."

"I think we ought to go away somewhere for a couple of days and concentrate really seriously on making love."

"I think that's a very good idea. Do you know, I've never made love to a bald woman before."

"Haven't you?" Maria looked at him in mock-surprise. "I thought you'd done everything, Jack Tarrant."

"Not quite everything."

"Apparently . . ." she sidled close to him and whispered in his ear – "it's rather *special* with a bald woman . . ."

"Oh? And which side of the family did you get that fascinating snippet of information from – the bishop or the actress?"

"That'd be telling." Maria giggled deliciously. "Mind you, the answer might surprise you. My father did have quite a varied life before he became a bishop, you know."

"Anyway, as I say, I approve whole-heartedly of your suggestion. And where do you propose we go for this forty-eight hour orgy?"

"Well, I thought maybe . . . one of those nice Country House hotels?"

"Erm . . . No, Maria. No, I don't think so."

She giggled again and, as she did so, the bedside lights suddenly came on.

"Power's been restored," said Jack. "Puzzel Manor's getting back to normal."

Maria looked at her watch. "Better pack, I suppose."

"Yes. And I've got one or two things to do, as well."

"Oh?"

He took from his pocket the crumpled sheet of paper on which he had drawn the shieldgrid. "Fill in the rest of this, for instance . . ."

And he filled in the answer to the puzzle Trudy Bastable had handed to him in the ice-house.

Maria Lethbury was transferring clothes from the chest of drawers to their suitcase when she noticed that Jack Tarrant had taken out a clean sheet of paper, on which he was working with a ruler and felt pen.

"What're you doing?"

"Passing the time."

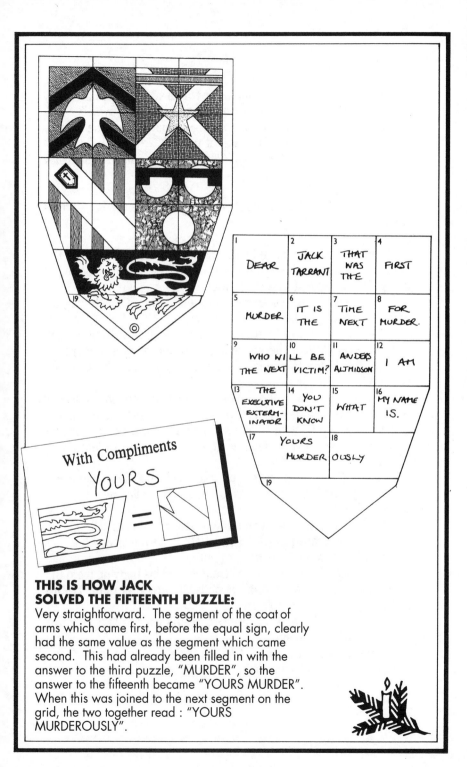

1 DEAR	2 JACK TARRANT	3 THAT WAS THE	4 FIRST
5 MURDER	6 IT IS THE	7 TIME NEXT	8 FOR MURDER.
9 WHO WILL THE NEXT	10 BE VICTIM?	11 ANDERS ALTMIDSON	12 I AM
13 THE EXECUTIVE EXTERM- INATOR	14 YOU DON'T KNOW	15 WHAT	16 MY NAME IS.
17 YOURS MURDER	18 OUSLY		

19

With Compliments

YOURS

=

THIS IS HOW JACK
SOLVED THE FIFTEENTH PUZZLE:

Very straightforward. The segment of the coat of
arms which came first, before the equal sign, clearly
had the same value as the segment which came
second. This had already been filled in with the
answer to the third puzzle, "MURDER", so the
answer to the fifteenth became "YOURS MURDER".
When this was joined to the next segment on the
grid, the two together read : "YOURS
MURDEROUSLY".

"Hm?"

"Just struck me that, having been tortured by fifteen of Trudy Bastable's puzzles, it's about time I set one of my own."

He continued ruling lines and inking in spaces until the walkie-talkie buzzed again. Maria picked it up.

"Helicopter approaching. We'll lower someone down to help pick up the wheelchair."

"Thank you."

"Perfect timing," said Jack, as he screwed the top back on his pen.

The helicopter once again hovered on the lawn. Maria took the suitcase and Jack wheeled himself out of the Yellow Room and along the corridor to the front door.

Two gumbooted uniformed policemen had been winched down and stood ready to help.

In the hall of Puzzel Manor a considerable farewell committee had gathered. All of the surviving staff and guests (except, of course, for Trudy Bastable and her brother) were there to see them off.

Graceful goodbyes and thank-yous were spoken, together with insincere look-forward-to-seeing-you-again-some-times. Apparently, the sudden thaw meant there was a good prospect that all the guests who wanted to would be able to leave that afternoon.

"Think it'll be easier if we take you and the wheelchair separately, Mr Tarrant sir," said one of the policemen.

"Fine."

"If I help you out, can you stand just for a moment?"

"No!" Maria interposed quickly. "He can't possibly –"

"Yes," said Jack. "Just for a minute."

And he did. His strong arms straightened his body up from the chair and, for the briefest of seconds, he stood upright, before collapsing against the policeman.

But, as he collapsed, he grinned triumphantly. "I'll make it, Maria. I *will* walk again."

"I know," she said, and a tear of pride glistened in her eye. "They'll never beat you, Jack Tarrant."

184

"Erm, excuse me, could I just have a word before you go . . . ?"

It was Roddy Stout. In spite of his obvious satisfaction that the Christmas Break had been completed without major disruption to his guests, he was looking slightly perplexed.

"Of course."

The hotelier came forward and whispered in Jack's ear. "Look, I'm still a bit confused, old man . . ."

"About what?"

"Well, these, er, murders. I mean, I gather that Trudy Bastable, of all people, was involved . . ."

"Yes. With her brother."

"But who is her brother?"

"Ah," said Jack. "I see what you mean. Well, that's very simple. The answer's on the table in the Yellow Room."

"Oh," said Roddy Stout, a bemused expression on his florid face. "Thank you."

The proprietor went straight to the Yellow Room, and found the sheet of paper Jack Tarrant had left on the table.

Roddy Stout studied it and looked totally blank. Puzzles weren't his kind of thing.

His gaze shifted to the window, in the forlorn hope of finding help.

But it was too late. All he could see was the diminishing outline of the police helicopter, flying Jack Tarrant and Maria Lethbury away from Puzzel Manor.

THE CHRISTMAS CRIMES AT
PUZZEL MANOR - HOPE YOU
COULD CONTRIVE TO SOLVE
EVERY ONE OF THEM!